TEXAS HELLTOWN

Texas Helltown

Jason Manning

DEDICATED TO

Ray Lake Manning,
my father;
an honest-to-God cowboy

"Courage is a man who keeps on coming on."
—L.H. McNelly Captain, Texas Rangers

Contents

COMANCHE AMBUSH

Riding through the dry dusty plain, the Comanche horde quickly drew within range and they fired. The rangers dealt death quickly with their new repeating Colts, but True relied on his .53-caliber, single-shot Hawken long gun to do his killing. Warrior after warrior fell under the sharp hooves of fast ponies as he made one well-placed shot after another.

But, as he was reloading, True glimpsed the shadow of a mounted Comanche on the high bank directly above them, ready to let loose an arrow. With ramrod still in the barrel, True aimed his weapon and fired. The heavy iron rod cut through the smoke-filled air and pierced the Indian in the neck, flying clean out the back in a spray of blood. The Comanche's pony panicked, rearing to the right and hurling the dead warrior down the rocky embankment.

Without a second to waste, True threw down his now useless Hawken, grabbed his pistol, and started firing.

1

Early one morning, True Bowen went hunting, a couple of miles north and west of the home place.

That was the day the Comanches came calling.

He left King George, the mule, at the edge of a big grove of Spanish and live oaks, proceeding into the bosky on foot. He knew how to move quietly through the brush. The same could not be said for King George.

Wild turkey were carrying on way back in the woods, so when he found the spring seeping through the limestone ledges of a shallow draw, he decided to settle down and wait for the big dumb birds to come to water.

At nineteen he was a full-grown man, tall and on the lanky side, broad of shoulder, and lean of hip. His eyes were blue, his auburn hair close-cropped. Years of farming had put iron in him.

Hot Irish blood ran strong in True's veins. He was the second son of Lake Bowen, Mississippi sharecropper turned Texas man of property. His older brother was named Chauncey, but most everybody called him Chance. The Bowen boys could whip their weight in wildcats, and their donnybrooks were already legend in the Guadalupe River country.

Two years back, in 1838, the Bowens had left a sharecropper's cabin on the banks of the Tallahatchie and headed west for the promised land of Texas. Two years before that, Texas had won its independence from Mexico and set itself up as a Republic, offering all the land a man could handle to get more folks to come out and put down roots.

Land with thick groves of trees and wide fields of graze, chock-full of rivers and streams, and fertile beyond the wildest dreams of a sodbuster. It was said a man could stick nails in the ground and grow himself a handsome crop of kingbolts.

Settled back now in a thick tangle of persimmon, his Hawken rifle across his knees, True felt mighty grateful to Chance. Back home, Chance had never taken to plowing and planting. "My hands fit better round a muzzle-loader than a middle-buster" was his own personal and oft-repeated declaration of independence. Leaving home in '36 to aid the Texans in their fight for freedom, he had crossed the Sabine too late. A month earlier, Sam Houston and a ragtag bunch of frontiersmen had whipped Santa Anna and a well-trained Mexican army at San Jacinto.

But Chance had stayed in Texas, and written letters home urging his father to pull up stakes.

The letters stoked the fire of westering in Lake Bowen. Chance told of Texas like it was a land of milk and honey. A place where a man could be whatever he wanted to be, if he was willing to work hard to make it, and fight hard to keep it. For Lake, Texas was a dream come true, the promise of a real future for his children—and their children.

True understood why his father caught "Western fever" so bad. A man needed to know the home he built and crops he grew belonged to him, not some high and mighty landlord who sat back and lived the good life thanks to the back-breaking labor of others. A man could never feel like a whole man until he knew the sweat and blood he spent was spent for his own future, and the future of his children.

Two years since, and True could still vividly remember the day the Bowen clan had loaded themselves and their few belongings into an ox-drawn wagon and headed for Texas. He remembered it had dawned bright and clear. Every drop of morning dew had flashed like liquid silver in the sunlight. The air had been pine scented, tasting like spring water with each breath. Mississippi had put on her best clothes, like she was trying to get them to change their minds about leaving her. All for naught; though he had not yet laid eyes on her, Texas was Lake Bowen's mistress.

Lost in pleasant memories, True jumped as something came crashing through the brush.

His first thought was that it had to be one of those wild Spanish mossbacks. The black cattle were thick as fleas all over Texas. He couldn't imagine anything smaller making such a big noise.

But it was no *ladino* charging clumsily through the bosky. It was Will Klemmer.

Will's clothes were torn. His complexion was ghost-white. Tripping over his big feet, he crashed into a tree trunk and then went flailing off in another direction. He was blind with fear, running away from something that had scared him badly.

Will was the son of Hans Klemmer, the Bowens' only neighbor for twenty miles in any direction. A couple of years younger than True, Will was a strong, strapping man, and True figured anything that could scare him had to be pretty frightening.

"Will," True yelled, standing up in full sight.

Will threw one quick look over his shoulder, let out a howl that turned True's blood to ice water, and ran.

True took off after him and, quick as a hair trigger, closed the gap. Dropping the Hawken at the last minute, he jumped on Will's back, hooked a leg, and brought him down.

Will clawed and kicked and twisted and finally pitched True off. True bounced right up, lowered his head, and hit Will full tilt in the breadbasket as he rose to commence running again. Klemmer bent over and went down hard, six feet from where True hit him. Wheezing air in and grunting it out, he sat there, stunned. Fists clenched and chin tucked, True stood over him, ready for more.

"What in tarnation's wrong with you, Will?"

Will was shaking like a dead leaf in a north wind, cutting hunted eyes this way and that. He stammered some, getting it out.

"Co … Co … *Comanches!*"

Half-yell and half-whimper, it didn't do True Bowen's nerves any good at all.

"Keep your voice down," he urged quietly.

He ran back to retrieve the Hawken. Returning to Will, he sat on his heels, looking and listening just as hard as young Klemmer.

"If they're chasing you, I sure can't tell it."

"I-I don't know. Maybe they ain't."

"Why'd you run from me?"

"Don't know," Will said again, sheepishly. "Didn't take a long enough look to see who you were, I reckon."

"What happened?"

All of a sudden, Will screwed up his face. He rolled over on his belly and began to cry.

In time he sat up, wiped his face with the sleeve of his thicket-torn homespun shirt, and pulled himself together.

"Pa told me I could go huntin' this morning, so I set out before first light. Hadn't gone far and I heard shouting. So I run back and … and seen them. The cabin was burning, the Comanches were everywhere. Lordy, True, there must've been a hunnerd of 'em."

True felt cold clean through.

"I was gonna try to get to your place," added Will.

"You were headin' the wrong way."

"God A'mighty, True! I was scared to death!"

"Where's your rifle?"

"I-I must've dropped it." Will was on the verge of tears again. "God, True! My folks … they must be …"

True felt his eyes start to burn. He knew the Klemmers well, and he felt sorry for Will.

"Come on," he said gruffly. "We've got to get to my folks before the Comanche do."

In one of his letters, Chance had mentioned the Comanches, and expressed his intention to join up with a bunch of tough-as-nails Texas fighters called the Rangers. The Rangers were sworn to protect settlers from the Comanches.

Of course True had dreamed of joining his brother and becoming a great Indian fighter. But with Chance gone, Lake Bowen had needed True's help, first with the move to Texas, and then in the building of the cabin and the raising of the crops in their new home. Lake Bowen was not the kind of father who tried to hold his sons against their will, but True had always felt it was his bounden duty to stay close and lend a hand. His younger brother, Ernest, was only nine, and had always been on the frail and sickly side. His mother, Emma, and his sixteen-year-old sister, Sadie, did their share, but starting a new life was hard work. Little Meg was barely a year old, and could do nothing well except caterwaul.

True's only thought now was to get home. His father needed him more than ever, with Comanches on the warpath. His mother and Sadie could shoot, but True was the best hand with a rifle in the Bowen family.

He led Will Klemmer out of the bosky. King George was right where True had left him. The mule didn't cotton to the idea of carrying double, but when he started kicking up some dust and braying louder than Gabriel's horn, True bent over and sank his teeth into one of the knobhead's ears. After that the mule settled down and behaved himself.

On the way, True couldn't help throwing plenty of anxious looks over his shoulder. He expected to see a swarm of screaming savages bearing down on them every time he checked their backtrail.

A quarter-mile from the Bowen cabin he heard the last sounds he wanted to hear.

Shooting, on the other side of a wooded rise.

Which meant it was coming from his home.

Sliding off the mule's bare back, he handed Will Klemmer the McCarty tied to King George's hackamore.

"Will, I leave it to you to get to Gonzales and fetch help."

"Gosh, True, that's … that's twenty miles!"

"Then why are you burning daylight, sittin' there all slack-jawed? Head straight thataway and you'll come to Ford's Ferry. From there you'll have the road to take you on into town."

Will listened to the shooting a minute, and turned white as a boiled shirt.

"Come with me, True."

"Pa needs my help, Will. Now you get on!" He slapped King George's rump hard enough to hurt his hand, and the mule lit out like it thought it was a thoroughbred racehorse.

The Hawken in his white-knuckled grip, True went loping up into the woods on the rise.

2

Coming out of the trees on the other side of the hill, he caught his first glimpse of the home place. What he saw stopped him dead in his tracks.

Comanches were everywhere, swarming like ants on a just-kicked mound. Most of them were mounted, and while he didn't take time to count, True reckoned there were forty of them, all told.

The cornfield was trampled. They had killed Dooley, the old july hound, and were running off Queen Anne, the other mule. They were also trying to steal Big Blue, but the ornery milk cow wasn't moving fast enough to suit them, and True arrived in time to watch them shoot her full of arrows.

Worst of all, they had set fire to the roof of the cabin. The pine shingles were burning furiously. A black column of smoke lifted into the blue summer sky.

Several Indians, dead or dying, were strewn on the grass slope in front of the cabin. Others milled about it, filling the air with war cries and shooting arrows. The cabin's windows were shuttered, and the walls were made of pine logs a foot thick, so arrows weren't going to have much effect. True saw only a couple of Indians with rifles.

A barrel emerged through a gunslot in one of the front window shutters, and a puff of white powdersmoke came out of it. A Comanche somersaulted off his painted warhorse. He hit the ground hard and never moved again.

True realized his folks couldn't stay holed up in the cabin much longer, and that once they came out they were done for. The Comanches knew this, too.

There was no help for him of his family closer than Gonzales, and True calculated it would take Will Klemmer four hours at least to get to town. The Bowens were on their own.

True started running toward the cabin. He had gone ten strides when a Comanche warrior spotted him.

The Indian was coming out of what was left of the cornfield. He had a war lance in one hand, a round hide shield on the other arm. Except for a breechclout, he was naked as a jaybird. His face was painted carmine red. A single eagle feather dangled from a small leathern disc braided in his hair.

True saw all this clearly and in a heartbeat, as the Comanche came out of the corn with smoke and flame shooting up behind him—they were putting the crop to the torch. He was the first Comanche True Bowen saw up close. And the first man True killed.

The warrior gut-kicked his wiry pony and let out a hoarse scream. The horse jumped like a jackrabbit and came pounding down on True, snorting and lathering like a critter straight out of the Devil's stables.

True spun to face the charge, the Hawken leveled at the hip. Squeezing the trigger was a reflex. He had neither the time nor the presence of mind to aim. The half-ounce ball caught the brave in the neck. The impact hung him up in the air and the painted pony galloped right out from under him. He landed in a broken heap, rag-doll limp.

Expecting the whole Comanche nation to be down on him now, True cast a quick look all around. But nary a one was paying him any mind that he could tell, because at that moment his father stumbled through the cabin door in a thick drift of gray-black smoke.

A half-dozen warriors went for him. Lake Bowen killed one with a rifle shot and hammered another off his horse, using the rifle like a club.

Two arrows struck Lake in the chest. He staggered back against the cabin wall. More arrows hit him, all at once, pinning him to the wall like a pelt staked out to dry.

A warrior jumped from his pony and stepped in, grabbing Lake's hair, knife in hand.

Emma came through the smoke billowing out of the door. She put a cap and ball pistol to the scalp-hungry redskin's head and pulled the trigger. One of the mounted Comanche drove his lance through her.

True saw the head of the lance come out his mother's back.

Screaming himself hoarse, he crashed through what was left of the cornfield. He ran through patches of fire, and didn't even notice he was getting burned.

He reloaded the Hawken as he ran. It was so much second nature to him that he didn't have to think about what he was doing. Powder, ball, patch, tamp all that down and then pull the hammer back and thumb the copper cap into place.

He had a long way to go, and was only just emerging from the blazing cornfield, clothes half-burned off blackened skin, when a warrior came out of the cabin with Ernest impaled on a lance.

The Comanche was hardly straining as he held True's younger brother aloft. Frail little Ernest had never weighed in at much; now he was being hoisted like a suckling pig on a roasting stick.

Meg was next. The warrior who brought the infant out tossed her to one of his mounted brethren. This one threw her to another. A half-dozen savages hurled her back and forth among themselves like a jug of corn liquor. The more Meg screamed the louder they laughed.

As True churned up the long slope, one of the warriors missed his catch, and Meg fell to the ground. The Comanches milled their prancing ponies around, howling so loudly they didn't hear True yelling at the top of his lungs. Trampled beneath unshod hooves, little Meg finally stopped screaming.

Pulling up, True brought the Hawken to his shoulder and fired into the pack of mounted Comanche in front of the burning cabin.

The bullet knocked one of them forward onto his pony's neck. The horse jumped sideways and the dead Indian slipped to the ground.

The rest of the pack noticed True for the first time. They were getting their horses turned to ride him down when another warrior came out of the cabin and cut loose with a triumphant cry as he dragged Sadie into the light of the bloody day.

The mounted bunch looked around, saw what their colleague had found, and started yelling even louder than before. They were pulled twixt pillar and post then—between killing True and getting their hands on Sadie.

True sensed they were arguing among themselves concerning who was going to do what. He put everything he had left into racing up that grass-covered rise. His legs and lungs were aching. The sound of blood pounding in his ears deafened him, so the first he knew of trouble coming at him from behind was the feel of the earth trembling beneath the thundering hooves of a hard-galloping horse.

He looked back and saw the warrior riding down on him.

Sadie was fighting like a wildcat as more Comanches closed in on her. Laughing, they cuffed her around, and tore at her clothes until her plain brown gingham dress hung in tattered shreds on a slender, blooming body white as alabaster.

True turned to confront the warrior. He caught a glimpse of deerskin leggins, breechclout, moccasins, bronze shoulders as wide as a doubletree, two eagle feathers in long, wind-whipped black hair. The Indian wore a neckpiece that appeared to be the jawbone of a wolf, teeth intact, tied to a rawhide thong. He carried a war lance, and seemed intent on driving it into True.

True hadn't had time to reload. Getting a good two-handed grip on the barrel, he braced himself and swung with all his might. The rifle struck the lance, deflecting it. But not enough.

A searing pain turned True's world black streaked with crimson.

The last sound he heard was Sadie's scream.

When he came to, True heard a meadowlark's song, the jangle of bit chains, a man's cough, hawk, and spit. He opened his eyes and gazed at a darkening sky striped with mare's tail painted in the orange and purple colors of sunset. He had time enough to notice how cold it was, and, remembering this was August, wondered at that. Then he tried to drag air into his lungs, and pain washed over him. He heard someone speak, and the man sounded far away.

"Well I'll be. The younker's alive. Who would've thought?"

He pried his eyes open again. It might have been a minute later, or an hour. He wasn't sure.

Chance leaned over him.

"Don't you go and die on me, True."

"I won't," said True.

Chance looked terrible. His complexion was ash gray, his cheeks hollow. His eyes were peculiarly bright, and seemed to have receded deeper into their sockets.

"True," he whispered, his voice ragged, "I can't find Sadie. Did they... did they take Sadie?"

Something wet slipped out the corner of True's eye and into the hair above his ear. That one got away from him. He kept the other tears corralled. Then he tried to get up, and almost passed out again.

"Rest easy," said Chance. "You're bad hurt. Hell, True, you're half-killed."

True raised his head slowly, and looked at the red-painted lance jutting from his side, halfway between rib cage and hipbone. The head of the lance had gone all the way through that fleshy part and into the ground. He was pinned to the earth, soaking it with his blood.

"I reckon they left him for dead," said someone whose voice True failed to recognize.

"We can't stand around here and wait for him to cross the river."

Another voice, but this one was familiar to True. Where had he heard that voice before? Trying to think, to even stay awake, was awfully hard. Didn't seem to be much profit in it. Just a whole lot of pain. True closed his eyes and began to drift away from the pain.

Chance slapped his cheeks.

"Don't you die on me, boy."

"I won't die," True managed to get out. "I just need to rest...."

"Stay awake."

"Private Bowen, we must press on after the Comanches." That familiar voice again. "They're only an hour or two ahead of us. We have spent precious time burying the dead."

"I'm mighty glad you didn't say we wasted the time," said Chance flatly, in a tone of voice that True knew spelled trouble for somebody.

"I'll leave Sergeant Hule behind. He's wounded, and can't hardly ride. He'll watch out for your brother. If we push hard, we might catch those damned copperbellies. Then we'll come back here. If your brother dies before then, Hule can bury him with the rest of your folks."

"Captain Steelman, I can't leave my brother when he's like this."

Steelman. Now True remembered.

Last Christmas, Chance had come home and stayed through the New Year. He'd brought a man with him—a Ranger captain named Ben Steelman.

Steelman was a living legend, a war hero and Indian fighter, a man of sharp features and flinty, killer-gray eyes. He dressed like a preacher and sported an iron gray goatee and a sweeping mustache. He was Chance's commanding officer.

The Bowens had felt right proud to have Captain Steelman as their guest, and tried to make him feel at home. He was courteous in a hollow way—a melancholy man with half-hearted smiles, when he smiled, which wasn't often.

True remembered that Christmas Eve dinner. Chicken and dumplings, English peas, ham and gravy, cornbread and butter, blackberry cobbler, cool buttermilk and coffee. Funny, how he could remember it so vividly. He could close his eyes and see his family sitting around that table....

Chance was slapping him again.

"I said stay awake, True, dammit."

True opened his eyes again. "Stop beatin' on me," he mumbled, getting mad.

"Private Bowen," said Steelman now, "in all the time you've ridden with me, you've not once given me cause to regret it Don't forget you swore an oath as a Ranger. You will obey my orders and mount up. I need every able-bodied man with me when I catch up to those hostiles."

"Go on, Chance," said True. "Go on and get Sadie back. I'll hold on here."

With a curt nod and a stricken look, Chance wrenched himself away from True's side. True knew it was hard on Chance, leaving him in this condition. It was just as hard for him, lying there all stove up, unable to ride with his brother to get their sister back.

He listened to the sound of horses galloping away. Another man came to kneel beside him and bend over into his line of sight. His eyes, deep in the shadow of a jutting brow, were as black and friendly as the twin barrels of a scattergun. His face was craggy and remote. When he spoke, his voice reminded True of a hot dry wind.

"Name's Hule. True Bowen, you want to live or die?"

The blunt question surprised True full awake.

"I got a choice?"

"Hell, yes. Most times you do. The lance went clean through your side. The Comanch' what tried to kill you did a poor job."

"I remember … he wore a wolf's jawbone. …"

Hule nodded. "Ol' Black Wolf his own self. Mean sonuvabitch. He's the leader of that damned Yamparika raiding party what done for your folks. And a good half-dozen other families further up the Guadalupe. We've been on their trail for the last two days. But they were moving too fast for us to get in front of 'em and turn 'em aside. Damned shame, but what's done is done. Now, about this lance. I can get it out. And maybe mend the hole before you bleed to death. But it'll hurt. A hurt like none you've known before. So that's why I ask. Some men would rather die than hurt like that."

"I won't give up. Not till Sadie—"

"That would be your sister. I reckon the bucks will use her pretty hard, if they haven't already. So she's good as dead. Don't worry your mind over her. This is between you and that lance. I've got a damned Comanche arrowhead in my thigh, and I ain't in no mood to trouble myself with you if you aim to go and die anyhow. So tell me straight. I'd just as soon go over yonder and find a good tree to lean up against and have me a chew of tobacco."

"If it ain't too much trouble," True said sharply.

Hule nodded and set right to work.

First, he rolled True over onto his side. That sent True's world into a spin. He gave True a piece of rawhide to bite down on, and then began to cut at the shaft of the lance with his Arkansas Toothpick. He tried to hold the lance steady, but every sliver of wood he whittled cost True dearly.

After carving a notch two-thirds of the way through, Hule broke the long part of the shaft off and threw it aside. True's eyes about popped out of his head, and he made a few unmanly noises over the rawhide, but he stayed conscious. He figured if he didn't, Hule would leave him to drift away into that sleep from which no man awakes, just so he could have a chew.

This left a short piece of the lance in True, with the stone head protruding out his back. Hule grabbed hold of the head and gave a quick hard pull that drew what was left of the shaft cleanly out of True's side.

True went out like a match in a strong breeze.

He wasn't out long—there was still a shred of daylight left in the sky. It felt like Hule had poured a whole gallon of turpentine into his wound. Turned out it wasn't turpentine, but gunpowder. Then Hule flicked a strike-anywhere to life on his thumbnail and set the black powder aflame.

True saw a puff of white smoke, and let go a howl any redbone hound would have been proud of.

3

Next thing True knew, night had fallen. His whole body was one solid block of pain. On top of that, he was feeling mighty cold again. He would have sworn on a tall stack of Bibles that a blue norther had blown in. His teeth were chattering louder than dice in a shook cup.

Hule had built a small fire, and True crawled closer to the heat. He covered about six inches of ground and stopped, too exhausted to continue.

The Ranger walked over. He was limping badly. His thigh wore a tight dressing. He was carrying a blanket, with which he covered True.

"Don't waste your time and energy getting any closer to the fire, Bowen," he advised. "You'll be burning up in a minute. You've got a fever."

True realized that Hule had dressed his wound, as well. The dressing was as tight as a woman's whalebone corset around his midsection.

"You don't look too good yourself, Hule."

"Don't wonder." The sergeant held out his hand. In the palm was an arrowhead, caked with dried blood. "I been trying to dig this feller out of my leg for the past hour. Left in much longer and I would've lost the whole leg, I reckon."

"When did it happen?"

"Yesterday. Stumbled on a wounded buck. Black Wolf had left him behind. He was too bad hurt to travel. Not bad hurt enough to keep him from letting a few arrows fly before I converted him."

True glanced at the fire. "You reckon Comanch' might see that?"

"They're long gone, Bowen. We won't have any redskin visitors tonight. Though were we to, I wouldn't complain. Killin' a Comanch' or three always improves my disposition."

True thought it would improve his own disposition to do the same.

They were on the long slope, where he had fallen, about fifty yards shy of the charred remains of the Bowen cabin. He closed his eyes against the sight.

As Hule had forewarned, he suddenly began to feel hot. He threw aside the blanket and asked for water, and Hule fetched a canteen. The Ranger allowed him only a sip. True could have drunk the Guadalupe dry.

"Hang in there," said Hule. "Right soon you'll be feeling as cold as a week-old tamale." He looked True over, and shook his head. "You're a holy mess, son."

"Obliged for your getting that lance out of me."

"Don't mention it."

"You'd rather be after the Comanch' than here wet-nursing me."

"I'druther, sure enough. But I weren't fit for hard riding with my leg."

"Think they'll catch up with the Indians?"

"Ain't no way of knowing."

They lapsed into moody silence. True kept thinking about Sadie. His sister had always been pretty as a picture. Her long hair was a rich brown, like mahogany. Her eyes were cornflower blue. She was a smiler, always in good cheer. A hard worker, too. She seldom complained or uttered a cross word.

He and Sadie had been the best of friends for as long as True could remember. She understood him. He would sometimes get into moods that would puzzle everyone else. But never Sadie. She always knew what he was thinking, what was troubling him. He never had a way with words, and could seldom express his feelings. Sadie did that for him, and was never off the mark by much.

Back in Mississippi, True recalled, the landholder's son had made a habit out of coming by the Bowen place, on some pretext or other, just to get an eyeful of Sadie. True was mighty protective and, on one occasion, had blackened the feller's eye when he had grown so reckless as to express his passionate feelings to Sadie, and with True in earshot. Sadie had just laughed. She was full of laughter and a love of life. Nothing could weigh down her heart.

True felt his own heart twist as he wondered what had become of her.

"You get a good look at the raiders, Bowen?" asked Hule suddenly.

True nodded, too miserable to speak.

"You seen any Comancheros with 'em?"

"Comancheros?"

"Yeah. Maybe a Mexican with a hook where his left hand used to be? Or a white man?"

"A white man? Riding with Comanches?"

"There are some low enough to do it. I can think of one right off. A murderin' bastard name of Quill Eason."

Sitting on the other side of the fire from True, Hule cut a quid off a plug of chewing tobacco with his knife. Chewing, he stared grimly off into the darkness.

"Sounds like you've got something against this Eason," remarked True.

Hule fastened those bleak gun-barrel eyes on him.

"There were these two young fellers, who fancied themselves hardcase desperadoes of the first order. They rode into Goliad one day and shot down a banker man named Rutherford. Killed him as he was walking down the street. It was their ill luck I happened to be in town that day. I shot one of 'em. Judd Eason was his handle. Younger brother to Quill, who got clean away. Judd, he hung on to life for a spell, though he was bad hit, and more than once."

He spat a brown stream of tobacco juice. "Anyhow, we carried Eason into the *bodega* and laid him out on a table. I didn't have to send for the doctor, as he was already there, drinking breakfast as was his custom. That old cut-em-up said there was no point in trying to save the boy, as he was for certain dead. But I kept at him. So he commenced to working on Eason, trying to dig my lead out of the younker.

"A truly mortifyin' sight, Bowen, believe you me. Judd got to screaming and crying and carrying on. He begged me to get that likker-lapping sawbones to hell and away from him. To let him die easy. I couldn't do it. I told him, I says, 'Judd Eason, I can't let you go till you tell me where your brother Quill talked about runnin' off to after you boys killed Rutherford. So I guess I'll have to let the doc keep diggin' around in your innards with that dull knife and unsteady hand of his.'

"I tell you straight, hoss, I've seen less blood in a butcher's barn. I bet they're still scrubbing that saloon down. Finally ol' Judd could stand no more. He told me Quill had spoke of settin' out for the border country. No-man's-land. Chock full of cutthroat scum. So I bought the doc another bottle of breakfast, and we drank a toast as Judd Eason went in peace. Damn his soul to everlasting hellfire."

True stared at the Ranger. No way around it: Hule had tortured a wounded man without mercy or remorse, until that man had betrayed his own kin.

Whether Judd Eason was a murderer or not, what Hule had done seemed all the way wrong to True. What bothered him most was a gut feeling that Hule had enjoyed every minute of it.

"I set out to track Quill Eason," continued Hule. "Spent all last summer and fall, lookin' for him, up and down the Bloody Border. Heard he took up with a band of Comanchero mustangers led by Gancho. A man with one hand and an iron hook where the other one used to be. But I lost the trail. Captain Steelman gave me the leave to hunt Eason, but I had to be back in Goliad come winter. Besides, I had my wife to think about."

He fell silent. True listened to the crackle of the fire. Off in the woods a horned owl hooted. Hule's horse, hobbled downslope, whickered.

"How come you took the killing of that banker man so personal?" asked True after a while.

"He was my cousin. I come from Tennessee mountain stock, Bowen. The blood feud is right and proper from where I stand. I don't kill Eason, I haven't done right by the Hule clan. I can't rest until my cousin's death is avenged."

True looked perplexed, and Hule went on to try and explain further.

"Take your own case. After what they done to your folks, and to your sister, iffen you come up on a Comanch' are you going to shake his hand and pass the time of day, or are you going to kill him?"

True said nothing. Both men knew the answer.

Two mornings later, Steelman's Rangers returned.

What True wanted most to see was Sadie riding double with Chance. He prayed to God as he had never prayed before. But as they came, grim and silent through the sun-splashed timber beyond the burned cornfield, True saw no sign of her, and his heart sank. When Chance dismounted and walked toward him, the look on his brother's gaunt face hurt True twice as bad as that Comanche lance.

"What happened, Chance? Where's Sadie?"

He sat down, legs crossed Indian-style, and morosely shook his head.

"She's gone, True."

"Gone? Not dead. You don't mean …"

"No. Not dead, far as I know. The Comanches still have her. They got away."

"Not all of them," said Steelman, coming over. He gave True a cursory once-over. "Looks like you'll pull through. Count your blessings, Private Bowen. Least you didn't lose your entire family."

The memory of last Christmas and Steelman's visit came back strong to True. After that fine Christmas Eve dinner, they had all gathered round the English Square piano Lake Bowen had just brought home to his wife from San Antonio. The instrument had cost a lot of money, but the first two years of Texas had been good to the Bowens, and Lake had wanted to find some way to thank his wife for her leaving family and friends behind in Mississippi to help make his dreams come true.

With Emma Bowen's accompaniment on the Square, the Bowens had sung Christmas carols. Tone-deaf, True couldn't carry a tune in a potato sack, but that hadn't stopped him from wailing like a tomcat, much to everyone's amusement.

Captain Steelman hadn't joined the songfest True recalled looking over in the middle of a song to see the Ranger standing at a window, gazing bleak-eyed out into the cold black night. And True had wondered then if Steelman was hearing the faint screams of loved ones, if the screams they had uttered while being brutalized and murdered were still carrying, somehow, on the winter wind.

He wondered now if the captain still heard those screams.

"You can't give up, Chance," said True sharply. It seemed to him as though Steelman was saying, in so many words, that Sadie was as dead as Pa and Ma and Ernest and little Meg. Worse than that, Chance appeared to be accepting this outlook whole-hog.

"You don't understand," replied Chance woodenly. "They're halfway to the Cap Rock by now. Beyond's the Staked Plain. What they call the Llano Estacado. That's Comanche country. Thirty Rangers wouldn't have a prayer out there. Not ten times thirty."

"Your brother's right," seconded Steelman. "If it's any consolation, we ambushed and converted eight of the stinking savages. Best thing you can do, Bowen, is join up with us. Be ready for when they come again. Forget about looking for your sister. You'd never find her. You'd just get yourself killed. Just remember what they done to her and others in your family, next time you have a Comanche buck in your gunsights."

"I won't forget about looking for her!" yelled True. He was still too weak to get up, but that didn't stop him from trying.

Steelman shot a frosty look at him and turned brusquely away.

"We'll get you to a doctor, True," said Chance. "When you heal up, I think you ought to join the Rangers, like the cap'n says."

"Oh, I'll heal," promised True. "And when I do, I'm going after Sadie. You can give up if you want. But I won't."

"I can't let you go out alone. Think straight, True. It's just plain crazy. I won't let you do it."

"You'll have to kill me to stop me," replied True.

4

Chance stayed with True while Steelman and the rest of the Rangers rode on to Gonzales. The captain promised to send a wagon out to transport True back to town, as he could not possibly ride in his condition. It would be weeks before he could walk, much less sit a horse.

Hule went with his compadres. Now that he had the arrowhead out, and two nights' rest under his belt, he was fit to travel. The Rangers weren't going to burn the breeze now anyway, as their horses were bottomed out, so Hule figured he could keep up with no problem.

As neither of the Bowen brothers could abide being so near the burned wreckage of the cabin, or the fresh graves behind it on the crest of the hill, Chance went down into the woods and brought back cuts of cottonwood and willow to build a travois. He used the travois to haul True to the other side of the wooded rise.

While they waited for the wagon, Chance told of the fight with the Yamparika Comanche.

The Rangers had tracked thirty-four mounted, unshod ponies into a cedar brake near Bulverde Creek. Encircling the brake, they had charged in at dawn, guns blazing. Instead of thirty-odd Comanche, they'd found only ten. Two escaped. The rest were slain. There was no sign of Sadie. A careful search by morning light showed where the other hostiles had left the brake in the middle of the night.

"Whoever was leading that bunch is one wily so-and-so," said Chance. "He left those ten behind as a rear guard and slipped off in the dark of night with the rest."

"With Sadie, too," said True bitterly, hating Black Wolf for being so clever.

Chance put his defenses up. "We tracked 'em. But our horses were plumb tuckered out, True. By midday they had the blind staggers. Worst thing that could happen to us was to be put on foot way out yonder. So finally we had to turn around."

"I wouldn't have."

"No, I reckon you wouldn't have. I reckon you would've ridden on until your mount died under you. Then you would have walked till you couldn't take another step. Then you would've crawled till you couldn't move another inch. Then you would've died. And Sadie would be no better off than before. But at least you'd be dead."

True laid off. Later, he asked what Chance knew about men called Comancheros.

"Comancheros," muttered Chance, screwing up his face like he'd just bitten into a red pepper. "They trade with the Comanches. Mexicans mostly. A few renegade whites. A bad bunch. Texas don't like 'em, but sometimes we need 'em. Now and again the Comanche will try to ransom off their white captives. They'll use the Comancheros as go-betweens. And the Comancheros trade guns and whiskey and such to the Comanches in exchange for the loot the Comanch' gather on their raids."

"Where do they do all this trading?"

Chance shrugged. "Not sure. Talk is there's a full-blown Comanchero town way off somewheres on the Staked Plain. No one I know is sure where it might be. Or if it really exists. Folks sometimes refer to it as Helltown. And I reckon it must be that in spades, if it's full of Comanches and Comancheros."

As promised, Steelman sent a wagon out for True, and before long he was laid up in an extra room in the home of a Gonzales widow woman name of Brister.

The townspeople treated him like a gold-plated hero. Total strangers came calling to congratulate him on his escape from the savage Comanches. Some bore gifts. True got a whole new set of clothes. A brand new pair of boots. A Bowie knife. His room was garnished with more flowers than the widow woman's garden, and he was presented with a Hawken rifle, compliments of the whole town. It was much like the one the Comanches had made off with. The stock plate was inscribed with his initials in elaborate script. Along with the rifle came a bullet bag and powder horn, both full.

True was grateful for the gifts, and highly embarrassed by all the attention.

Will Klemmer came to visit, returning King George the mule. Will looked bad. Gaunt and listless, he scarcely resembled the big, robust fellow True had known before. His whole family had been slaughtered by the Indians, and he did not appear to enjoy drawing breath.

According to the doctor who kept a close watch on him, True's recovery was nothing short of miraculous. But there was really nothing very miraculous about it. The Widow Brister was largely and unwittingly responsible, much more so than the doctor's mustard plasters and black draught tonics. She fussed over True like a mother hen, until he could honestly bear no more. In a week he was sitting up. Three days later he was walking about. Ten days after that he begged Chance to break him out. The widow's kindness was unbearable.

Chance had mercy on him. Less than four weeks after arriving laid up in a wagon bed, True was riding King George out of Gonzales, with Chance, and heading north out of town.

They reached the Bowen place close to sundown. There wasn't much left. The cabin had burned to the ground. The crops were destroyed. While True had been recuperating, Chance had come out to put wooden crosses, bearing names and dates, on the graves, and he had covered the final resting places with rocks to keep the varmints away from the bodies.

"I tried to remember some words from the Good Book to say over them," he said, half-choking with emotion. "But I couldn't recall..." He coughed and sniffed and added, with real feeling, "Damn Comanches."

True turned and walked away.

Following, Chance said, "I reckon we can build another cabin, True. You and me. I admit I ain't much for farming, but you seem to have a real talent for it. I guess I ought to stick with what I know best, which is Rangerin'. But you could make something of this place. It's yours now, True. You can settle down here. That's what Pa would've wanted, I reckon."

Of a sudden, True stopped in his tracks, and listened hard. A warm summer breeze stirred his auburn hair and the tattered hem of the serape he had fashioned from Hule's blanket. Looking at the charred remains of the cabin, his blood ran cold, and a hard shudder racked him.

"True, are you all right?"

He nodded. "I can't stay here, Chance," he said, hollow-voiced. "I just can't. I can still hear little Meg screaming. I swear I can."

"Good God, True," whispered Chance raggedly. "Don't say such things."

True stumbled forward.

Chance held back a minute, throwing a bleak look over his shoulder at the graves.

True broke into a run, making for their mounts, King George and his brother's tall sorrel, tethered to a burnt-black piece of roof pole resting on the ground among the rubble of the cabin.

"True!"

The Bowie knife was twelve inches of brass-ribbed blade with a buckhorn handle, carried in a belt sheath. True used it to slash the sorrel's reins and at the same time pulled the mule's tether free.

He jumped into the saddle without touching boot to stirrup.

The sorrel began to turn and True slapped his hat across its face, letting out a yell that set King George to crow-hopping. The sorrel broke into a hard gallop, kicking like a bronc.

He struck the mule between the ears with his fist, and King George settled down, took off at a spine-jarring lope that wasn't fit to look at but which covered ground in a hurry.

"True! You crazy fool! What are you doing?"

True looked back.

Chance was running, and falling quickly behind.

"True, for God's sake…"

"I'm going to get Sadie back, Chance!"

"Stop, dammit!"

"I'll be back, Chance. I'll be back with our sister."

Chance quit running and threw his hat to the ground, cursing a blue streak and casting about for the sorrel, but the horse had gone over the backside of the hill.

True felt bad, doing his brother this way. He knew Chance was hurting, convinced like he was that True was all the family he had left.

But there lay the big difference between them. Chance had given up on ever seeing Sadie again.

True hadn't.

So he left Chance behind, with the burned cabin and the four graves on the rim. He looked back just that once, never again, then turned his gaze to the blood-red setting sun, the Bowie knife on his hip, the Hawken across the saddlebow, and a tough old mean-spirited mule beneath him.

Somewhere out there in the big wide-open was Sadie. Somewhere closer to the sunset. True wanted to call out to her, but of course she was too far away to hear. He wanted so much to let her know he was coming. So he tried to reach out with his thoughts. They had always been so close. Maybe now, as before, she knew what he was thinking.

Hold on, Sadie. Don't give up hope. I'm coming for you, Sis. I'm coming on.

5

The mustanger stumbled out of the cool darkness of the border town cantina. Swatting clumsily at a bluebottle fly that pestered his dark, stubbled cheek, he absently scratched his crotch and scanned the sun-blistered village square.

Hardly a stone's throw away, True Bowen pulled King George to a halt and sat the mule in the deep shade of a building that lined the road entering the square from the north.

The Mexican was a burly character. He had a pistol and knife in his belt, a rawhide rope and rolled Saltillo blanket angled across his barrel chest.

Pushing a sombrero's floppy brim out of his eyes, he tried to swagger across the rutted hardpack of the square. His destination seemed to be the well marking the center of the *zócalo*. He could not walk a straight line, and his swagger was more a stumble. True figured he was drunk. Had to be. He couldn't see any better than he could walk—he was unaware of True's presence.

As the mustanger reached the dappled shade of three scrawny mesquite trees flanking the well, a yapping dog scampered around the corner of an adobe hut, hotly pursued by a barefoot boy.

Working the hand crank to elevate the water-filled well bucket, the mustanger cursed the boy and the dog for making so much noise. The mutt laid back its ears and growled. The man made a threatening gesture and almost lost his balance. The dog backed off, and the boy caught him up and carried him to safety.

True had been searching for Gancho and his band of Comancheros for two months. In that time he had heard plenty about mustangers. About how they were generally a rough and law-less bunch. About how many of them were wanted men.

From one border town to the next he had traveled, asking after Gancho. Though it was apparent that many knew of the man, True seldom got a straight answer concerning his whereabouts. He could not pay for information, and few would give it out of the goodness of their hearts.

All he knew for certain was that Gancho and his mustang crew usually wintered somewhere along the Bloody Border. Waiting for spring, when many mustang mares foaled and the colt catch was at its best, they made themselves the unwelcome guests of some poor, isolated village.

The well bucket arrived, leaking through its warped slats. The mustanger used the wooden ladle tied to the bucket's bale, taking a few sips and then, throwing back his sombrero, dashing the rest of the bucket's contents over his head. Spluttering, he unbuttoned the fly of his grime-blackened leather trousers and relieved himself against the adobe bricks of the well.

A young woman emerged from one of the *casitas* facing the square. She carried a glazed clay water jug under one arm. Seeing the man, she pulled up. Leering, he shouted something at her.

True had learned only a smattering of the lingo the past two months, so he could make little sense of the Mexican's slurred remark, but the woman obviously did not find it the least bit charming. She fled back into the hut, pursued by the mustanger's bawdy laughter.

Drawing a long breath, True kicked King George into motion and rode on into the square. The mule broke into a teeth-rattling trot and snorted at catching the alluring scent of water. They had both gone all day without any.

Hearing the mule, the mustanger groped for the pistol in his belt.

True already had the Hawken rifle loaded and capped, lying across the saddlebow, hammered back. That a man entered a bor-dertown prepared for trouble was a lesson he had already learned.

When he saw the newcomer was just a young and solitary gringo, the mustanger relaxed, and left the gun in his belt. His eyes glittered with greed as he examined the mule, the Hawken, and the Bowie knife. Prizes many a border hardcase would gladly kill for.

Reaching the well, True checked King George and contemplated with suspicion the grin on the Mexican's coarse features.

"Beg pardon," he said, polite and poker-faced. "But your britches ain't closed."

The mustanger gave a jolt of surprise, hastily buttoned up, and tried to hide his embarrassment behind good cheer that rang false.

"*Buenos dias, amigo.* Step down. Rest yourself. You are much welcome. Have some of our water, *por favor.*"

"Mighty neighborly," said True.

Dismounting, he dropped rein leather to ground-hitch King George, then stepped past the Mexican and cast the bucket down. Its splash was punctuated by a sudden burst of laughter from inside the cantina. True glanced that way, then at the mustanger, who put more muscle into his counterfeit grin.

"My *compadres, amigo.* We too have had a hard ride. A man must take his pleasures when he can, no?"

"I reckon, if you say so."

Some people, mused True, were easy to read. This feller was one of those. True knew exactly what he was thinking. And exactly what he was aiming to try.

"You are a well-mannered *muchacho*," said the mustanger. "What brings a nice young man like you to Mexico?"

"We're some miles north of the Rio Bravo, ain't we?"

"Yes, that is so."

"Well, then, I reckon this here ground we're standing on rightfully belongs to the Republic of Texas."

"It is not always enough to claim something is yours, *gringo.* Sometimes you have to take it."

True nodded. Texas had claimed the river as its southernmost border after Santa Anna's surrender. Problem was, there weren't enough Texicans moved down here yet to make the claim stick.

"I'm looking for a man named Gancho," he said, turning his back on the mustanger to raise the well bucket.

Listening hard, he heard the knife whisper as the blade brushed the *mesteñero*'s belt in passing.

"What do you want with Gancho?" He was talking loud to hide any noise he made moving in.

"Want to cut a deal."

The man chuckled. "Gancho deals with men. Not *muchachos*. You have made a long trip for nothing. But I am glad you did...."

The bucket was within reach.

True laid hold of the bale and whirled, swinging the bucket for all he was worth. There was plenty of slack in the windlass rope, and he hit the mustanger right in the head. The man crumpled. True dropped the bucket and stepped on the other's knife hand. Bending down, he laid the Bowie knife against the Mexican's throat.

"Sir, I hope next time you'll have the decency to come at me from the front."

"Do not kill me, *por favor*. I ride with Gancho. He would be very angry if you killed me."

True drew back with the knife and stepped away.

Dripping wet, the mustanger regained his feet, rocking unsteadily. The swagger and friendly pretense were gone. His eyes were blank and lethal, like a sidewinder's.

True wondered then if he had made a mistake. If maybe he should have killed this one while he had the chance.

"How many friends you got in yonder?" he asked, nodding at the cantina.

"Six."

"Gancho? He in there, too?"

The mustanger nodded, glaring.

True grinned like a fool.

"Well, shucks. Ain't this my lucky day?"

He put the Bowie knife back in its sheath.

The mustanger considered reaching for his pistol. He took a long look at True, and decided to wait until Bowen's back was turned again.

"After you," said True.

The man turned toward the cantina. True swept up the reins and dragged King George along. The mule put up a fuss about leaving the well without first sampling its contents.

Following the mustanger across the sun-hammered alkali dust, True had sense enough to realize that he had stepped into a rattlesnake hole here.

But he couldn't help feeling mighty relieved. His search was over. He had found the Comancheros.

And that put him one step closer to finding Sadie.

The boy and his flea-bitten mutt stood in a narrow ribbon of shade at the corner of the cantina, watching the two men cross the hardpack. As the mustanger drew near, the dog laid back its ears, lowered its tail, and bared its yellow fangs.

Dogs, reflected True, were fine judges of character.

As he secured King George to a big iron ring set into the cantina wall, the mongrel made a threatening advance upon the mustanger. The Mexican aimed a quick and vicious kick, bowling the dog end-over-end. The mutt went yelping away, with the boy chasing after. The mustanger looked like he felt a whole lot better about things now.

True reacted without thinking, placing a well-aimed kick of his own. The mustanger hurtled headlong through the open doorway. True followed quickly. Once inside, he sidestepped and put his back to the wall.

The cantina looked like a half-dozen others he had visited in his search for Gancho. The uneven floor was hardpacked earth. The walls were bullet-pocked and fly-specked. The bar was fashioned from warped boards laid across a brace of barrels, along the rear wall. Tables and chairs cluttered the space between the front door and the bar. A single window with shutters opened allowed a shaft of late afternoon sunlight to pierce the smoky dimness. The place reeked of raw liquor, stale tobacco, and unwashed bodies.

True counted seven people in the room, aside from himself and the man he had just kicked. Four had the rough-at-the-edges look of Mexican mustangers. Two of these sat at one of the tables, playing a game of cooncan. A third, his chair propped against a wall, had a guitar in his lap. He was too busy consuming the contents of a wicker-cased jug to bother trying to coax a tune from the instrument's three remaining strings.

The fourth *mesteñero* sat at the table nearest the door. There was an iron hook where his left hand used to be. This, realized True, was the man Hule had spoken of. The man called Gancho.

Gancho looked tough enough to be the leader of hardcases like these Comancheros. In such a group, the most ferocious, ruthless, and cunning individual was *el jefe*.

He wore a red shirt, tucked into pants that in turn were tucked into black jackboots. A quirt of braided rawhide dangled from his belt. Though he was middle-aged, there wasn't an ounce of softness to him.

He was grinning across the table at his adversary in an arm-wrestling contest.

True pegged the other contestant as a local. A big-bellied, sweat-soaked, scared mountain of a man, twice Gancho's size. But size wasn't a factor; Gancho was going to win. Everybody knew that.

The last two occupants of the cantino stood behind the bar.

One was an Anglo. True figured this had to be Quill Eason.

The man flashed an easy grin.

The other was a girl. Pretty, with braided raven hair, dressed like a man.

True wanted to rest his eyes on her a while longer, but the Mexican he had kicked was rolling over and sitting up.

He was also pulling the pistol out of his belt.

Sweeping the Hawken down, True aimed the rifle at a spot right between the man's eyes.

At the same time, the cooncan players and the guitar man were coming up out of their chairs and going for their own weapons.

True thought, I have spent months looking for the Comancheros. Now I'm going to get killed for my trouble.

Distracted, the overweight local surrendered to the inevitable, and Gancho slammed his arm to the table, then leaped jubilantly to his feet.

"*Ojála!* I have beaten you, Raoul! I have always wanted to own a place such as this."

Raoul was the picture of dejection.

True took a hasty look around. The other mustangers had their guns pointed at him, and he had one of theirs dead to rights. Looked for all the world like they were an amen away from shooting holes in each other, and here was Gancho celebrating a little old arm-wrestling victory.

"I have lost all that I possess in this miserable world," moaned Raoul.

Gancho laughed. "I will grow tired of being a saloon-keeper before long, *amigo.* Then I will let you buy your business back from me. Until then, though, all drinks are on the house."

Raoul groaned.

"Beg pardon," said True.

Gancho, for the first time, seemed to take note of the standoff.

"Who are you?" he asked, in good English.

"Name's True Bowen. This feller says he rides with you. Says you'll be right put out with me if I kill him. But it's lookin' more and more like I got no choice."

Gancho stared with withering scorn at the man on the floor.

"What are you doing down there, Guerrero?"

"This *gringo* kicked me, *jefe.*"

Gancho gave True a closer look.

"Guerrero, this one looks like he has lived off a hard biscuit and a cup of water every day of his life. How could this have happened to a big, strong *hombre* like you?"

"He struck from behind."

True thought the accusation took some nerve on the part of Guerrero, seeing as how the mustanger had tried to bushwhack him not five minutes earlier.

"Is this true?" Gancho asked True.

"Can't deny it."

"Why did you kick one of my men?"

"He kicked a dog. I won't abide anybody mistreatin' a poor dumb animal like that."

Gancho looked bewildered.

"This man you kicked. He has killed many men. It strikes me as foolish to make an enemy of someone like this, just because he kicked a dog."

True nodded. "Could be I made a mistake. Pa always told me I had a hair-trigger temper. He used to say I'd jump into a fire without so much as a bucket of water."

Gancho sighed. "Sadly, Guerrero is not the forgiving kind."

"Well, I'm too derned proud to ask for forgiveness, anyhow. I can see you're right about him. So I reckon I'd best just shoot him and feel sorry about it later."

"These men," said Gancho, with a gesture including the other Comancheros, "they are friends of Guerrero's. They would not take kindly to your doing such a thing."

"You've just got to handle one problem at a time."

Gancho smiled.

"I like you, young man. And I like Guerrero. We have ridden together for many years. I would not want two men that I like shooting one another."

"Oh, we weren't going to shoot each other," corrected True. "*I* was going to shoot *him*."

6

G ancho threw back his head and laughed.

"Put away your rifle, True Bowen. We will leave this little misunderstanding behind us. No hard feelings. Have a drink with me. Sombra, tequila, *ahorita.*"

The woman behind the bar started around with the bottle in hand. She hesitated, seeing that True had not eased off, was still aiming the Hawken at the bridge of Guerrero's nose.

"I haven't heard you talk truce yet," said True.

"He will do as I say," assured Gancho.

"But, *jefe!* This bastard kicked me!"

"I know that. So what?"

"*Jefe,* he is one Tejano. We are many. We should kill him. He has a fine rifle, a good knife, and rides a strong mule."

"Don't feature we'll do any such thing," said Quill Eason.

Eyebrows hiked, Gancho glanced at Eason.

"Do you know him, Eason?"

"Nope."

"Then why do you take up for him?"

"Let's just say he reminds me of someone I once knew. Besides, you must admit he's got sand, comin' in here alone like he has."

Gancho peered at True. "My friend says you are *muy valiente.* How brave are you, gringo?"

"Not so much brave as lucky."

"A brave man makes his own luck. What are you doing here?"

"Looking for you, Mr. Gancho."

"Why?"

"I have to find a Comanche called Black Wolf. He took my sister and I want her back. I don't reckon I can find him all by my lonesome. So I thought you might help me."

Gancho looked at him for a long, speculative moment. Then he turned to face his men.

"Put away your *pistolas, amigos.*"

They obeyed. Guerrero relaxed, accepting defeat. True could sense, however, that Guerrero wasn't apt to forgive or forget.

"Come, sit at my table, True Bowen," said Gancho. "We will drink together. 'Cuss and discuss' as you Tejanos say."

True pulled back on the Hawken. Still sulking, Guerrero got to his feet and walked stiffly to the bar, where Quill handed him a bottle of painkiller.

Gancho sat down. True slacked into the chair vacated by Raoul, who had discreetly removed himself to a safer corner of the cantina. The seating arrangement suited True just fine. He could see everyone in the place and was only a long jump from the doorway.

The girl, Sombra, brought the bottle of tequila to the table.

She wore snug leather pants flaring below the knee to better fit over the boots encasing her small feet. A scarlet sash complemented her waist, and under her short brown jacket was a plain white *camisa.*

Lingering at the table, she looked at True with brazen brown eyes. True looked every which way but at her, uncomfortable beneath this bold scrutiny. He wasn't accustomed to such attention from young ladies.

Grinning like a fox, Gancho pushed the bottle across the scarred tabletop.

"Drink. Wash down the dust of a long trail."

"Much obliged," mumbled True, painfully self-conscious. "Fact is, I don't indulge."

"What? You are Tejano, no? I thought all Tejanos were big drinkers."

"I'm Texan, yessir, and proud to say so. But liquor don't agree with me."

Shrugging, Gancho took the bottle and swallowed a third of its contents before coming up for air. With a gasp he slammed the bottle down with such force that the table bounced off the ground and everyone in the place jumped. Except True.

Gancho leaned forward. "So you want to find Black Wolf? You want to rescue your sister? What makes you think I will help you?"

"Never hurts to ask."

"Maybe you have heard that Comancheros trade with the Comanche. That sometimes we serve as middlemen when Tejanos want to rescue loved ones who have been taken by the Komantcia. Sometimes we do. What do you have with which to buy your sister's freedom?"

"Like your man said. A rifle, a knife, and a mule."

Gancho snapped his fingers. Raoul delivered a cheroot. The Comanchero chieftain clenched the smoke between his teeth, watching True as Raoul scraped a lucifer on the tabletop and fired the tip. Puffing vigorously, Gancho settled back in his chair. True blinked as the biting blue smoke got into his eyes.

"That will not be enough," decided Gancho. "What else do you have?"

"Nothing. Thanks to the Comanches."

"No money?"

True shook his head.

"Black Wolf would not take less than ten horses for your sister, I feel sure."

"Ten horses?"

"I know Black Wolf, you see. Your sister. Is she pretty?"

"Yes."

"Then he will not easily part with her."

"Ten horses," muttered True, discouraged.

Gancho nodded. "Maybe more. You should understand something about Comanches and horses. To a Comanche, horses are like money. The more horses he has, the richer a warrior is. He can capture and break wild horses himself, although he prefers to steal them. Less hard work. Black Wolf himself may have as many as a hundred horses in his own remuda. But he will always want more."

"I haven't got ten horses."

"Then you should go home."

"I haven't got a home, either."

True glanced sidelong at the girl, who still stood by the table. Her brown eyes glowed with an honest compassion. True knew, then and there, that for some reason unknown to him, there was at least one among the Comancheros who was on his side.

"Tell you what," he said. "Mr. Gancho, you trade ten horses for my sister. Then I'll give you everything I've got in exchange for her."

Gancho chuckled. He looked over at his men, and they started chuckling right along with him. True's blood began to boil. This was his sister they were talking about.

"Maybe I'll take you up on the deal, True," said Quill Eason, speaking up loud and strong over all the merriment.

Gancho stopped chuckling. He glowered at Quill, then at True, his black eyes hooded.

"Go back where you come from, gringo."

"Just tell me where I can find Black Wolf, and I'll go."

"Black Wolf is Yamparika Comanche. The Yamparika, as do all the Comanche bands, call the Llano Estacado home. They move from place to place as easily as you would go from room to room in your own *casa*. There is no way to say for sure where Black Wolf's lodge stands today. Or where it will stand tomorrow."

"But he'll go to Helltown, sooner or later. Tell me where Helltown is."

"No Comanchero will ever tell you that."

True did a foolish thing then. He was desperate, because all along he had known that the Comancheros were his only real hope of getting to Sadie.

The Hawken lay across his knees. The hammer was still back. He shifted the rifle until it was pointed under the table at Gancho.

Standing beside the table, Sombra blocked this move from the sight of everyone else in the cantina. But Gancho knew, and so did she.

"Tell me where Helltown is," said True, low and soft.

Gancho's half-closed eyes glittered. True's guts twisted as he saw his mistake. This man would not be threatened. He would not back down.

Then Sombra spoke up.

"Bowen. I will help you."

"Be quiet," growled Gancho.

The knife came from somewhere under her jacket. In the blink of an eye the blade was pressed against Gancho's throat.

"Don't tell me what to do," she snapped, eyes flashing fire. "I am not yours to order around. You would do well to remember that."

"I forgot," said Gancho, quite still and forcing a smile, "whose blood runs in your veins."

True didn't trust that smile. Gancho was too proud to let anyone, especially a woman, put a knife to his throat and get away with it. Particularly in the presence of the other Comancheros.

When Sombra lessened the pressure of the blade, Gancho struck. He got her wrist and twisted. Sombra gasped at the pain. The knife fell to the floor. Gancho bent her arm in such a way that she had to double over and drop to one knee. To her credit, she didn't cry out.

Gancho began to come out of his chair, raising his hook as though to strike her.

True hit the underside of the table with the barrel of the Hawken, overturning it. The bottle of tequila went flying. Before it shattered on the hardpack, True was standing with stock to shoulder, a bead drawn on Gancho, his finger tightening on the trigger.

"Let go of the lady."

Once again the Comancheros started pulling artillery.

Looking down the barrel of the Hawken, Gancho made a sharp gesture that stilled his men.

"Now I remember," he said wryly. "You don't like it when dumb animals are mistreated." He let go of Sombra. She stood quickly, rubbing her wrist. The knife lay on the ground at True's feet. She bent to recover it, and for a minute he thought she was going to gut Gancho like a fish.

"Go ahead, Tejano," said Gancho. "Kill me. Shoot, or put the rifle down. I don't feel like standing here all day."

"I didn't come here to pick a bone with you," replied True. "My quarrel is with the Comanches."

"You give me your rifle, knife, and mule, and maybe I will let you live."

"Bold talk from a man about to die."

"There's a way to settle this," remarked Quill Eason, "without a lot of folks gettin' killed."

Gancho looked at him. True kept his eyes glued to Gancho.

"We're listening," said True.

"Bowen, you have a mighty peculiar way of asking for help. And you picked the wrong people to ask."

"Reckon I made a mistake. But I ain't leavin' without my possibles."

"These men hanker to kill you. I'm doing my level best to save your bacon."

"Mine ain't the only bacon in the fire."

"Gancho here doesn't think there's a man born who can best him at arm-wrassling. Why don't you two have at it? If you win, Bowen, you keep your gear—and your life. Lose, and you walk out of here. But you leave everything except the shirt on your back. Sound fair, Gancho?"

Gancho shrugged. "*Muy bien.*"

"He's agreeable because he doesn't think he can lose," said True. "If he *does* lose, what's to keep him from having a change of heart?"

"He'll keep his word," promised Quill. "He may be a thief and a killer, but he fancies himself a gentleman about it."

True realized he didn't have a choice. He had gambled, coming here, and he had lost. Either he accepted Eason's proposal, or prepared to meet his Maker.

And he wouldn't do Sadie a bit of good, were he buried in some dusty border-town bone orchard.

He lowered the Hawken.

"Reckon I'll have to take your word for that."

Eason came across from the bar and righted the table. Gancho picked the half-smoked cheroot up off the hardpack and clenched it between his teeth. He and True sat, planted their right elbows and clasped hands, flexing fingers to get the best possible grip.

The other Comancheros were grinning at True like he was tomorrow's dinner. True understood that Eason's game would get him out of here alive, and no more. After that, these men would hunt him down like a dog. That was guaranteed.

"Give the word," said Gancho.

Quill waited out the count of three. "Have at her, gents."

They set to. Gancho fixed a bright gaze on their clasped hands. True watched Gancho's face. The Comanchero was grinning over that smoldering cheroot. Their arms trembled with the fierce exertion.

A full minute passed. The place was so quiet True could hear flies buzzing. A bead of sweat snaked down his forehead and into his left eye, stinging like the dickens. True blinked it away.

Another minute. Gancho's aggravating grin tightened. Their arms were still absolutely vertical. Gancho had figured beating True would be no hill for a stepper. Now he was beginning to wonder. He was plenty strong. But True had years of plow-pushing behind him. Such work put power in a man's arm and shoulder muscles.

Another minute. Gancho's boot heel ground the hardpack. The cheroot's smoke hung thickly in the still air between them. Taking a deep breath, True exhaled slowly through thinned lips. The smoke stirred, drifting back into Gancho's face. Gancho blinked rapidly at the irritating sting of the fumes.

True's arm burned with white-hot fire from finger joints to shoulder. He ignored the pain, and put everything he had left into one tremendous effort. In astonishment, he watched Gancho's hand bend at the wrist. Gancho lost his leverage—and his grin. With a final surge, True slammed his opponent's arm to the table.

Gancho jumped to his feet. He spat the cheroot out of his mouth. His eyes, red and watering from the smoke, were filled with a cold and deadly fury. True couldn't read what was coming, but braced for the worst.

"No one has ever beaten me," said Gancho flatly.

"Well, you didn't have as much to lose as Bowen here," said Quill. "Sometimes desperation wins out over strength."

True rose and turned to Sombra.

"Ma'am, I'd be obliged for your help."

The way she was gazing at him made him feel uneasy.

"We will leave in the morning," she replied.

"Maybe now would be better," murmured Quill.

"He has won the right to do as he wishes," she snapped.

True's first inclination was to get while the getting was good. He scanned the dark, scowling features of the Comancheros—and changed his mind.

Once he walked out of the cantina, Gancho had kept his word. After that, all bets were off, and he was fair game.

Sometimes, the safest place to sleep was right alongside the thief.

"I reckon the morning will be soon enough."

"There's a hut out back," said Quill. "Corral for your mule."

True turned his back on them and walked out, into the red heat of the dying day, like he didn't have a care in the world.

All the while he was wondering if he would live to see the sunrise.

7

She crossed the hardpack in the purple dusk, carrying a plate covered with a piece of burlap. Pausing at the doorway of the adobe hut behind the cantina, she called the gringo's name. No answer. Night had already gathered inside the hut. She glanced at the mule, standing in the corral and watching her.

Coming around the corner of the hut, True walked up behind her and cleared his throat.

She spun, startled, and struck her arm against the wall. The plate was jarred from her hand. True caught it, but most of the food dumped out and fell on the ground.

"Awful sorry, ma'am. Was that meant for me?"

"You walk too softly," she scolded. Then she laughed. "We should go inside. It is not safe for you out here."

He followed her into the hut. Scraping a lucifer to life, he lit a candle set in a pewter cup on the trestle table. Over against one wall was a rope-slat bunk covered by a thin cornhusk mattress. Disturbed, field mice scurried in dark corners. True laid the plate on the table.

A moth-eaten wool blanket was rolled up on the bunk. Taking this, he used the handful of cholla spines he'd just gathered to tack it over the open doorway. The long, stout yellow spines were easy to push into the crumbling mudbrick.

"I didn't fancy myself a target against the light," he said when finished.

Sombra pulled the blanket aside and peered out.

"I'd be careful sticking my head out like that, were I you," cautioned True. "There's a man out there who might mistake you for me and shoot."

"What man?"

"Right now he's over at the corner of the cantina."

"I see no one."

"I haven't exactly seen him. But he's there, sure enough."

She dropped the blanket back into place and stared at him.

"How do you know this?"

True shrugged. "Just do, is all. 'Course, he'd have to be awful poor-sighted to mistake someone pretty as you for a buzzard-faced scarecrow like me."

She looked pleased. "You think I'm pretty?"

"Shucks, don't everybody?" True felt like he was in deep water and getting deeper, so he changed the subject. "You sure you know where Helltown is, ma'am?"

"Oh, yes. I know. I have lived there."

"You? Lived in Helltown?"

"Once." She looked away. "Years ago."

"How long will it take to get there?"

"You will need horses to trade, first."

"Where will I get horses?"

"We will get them together. I am a *mesteñera*. For years I have caught wild horses."

"I don't have much experience when it comes to wild horses."

"I will teach you. I am as good as any of the others. As good as Gancho himself. We will catch many fine horses, you and I. Then, in the spring, we will ride to Helltown."

"Spring? I can't wait till green-up!"

"The Comanches will winter on the plains. In the spring, Comanchero freighters leave Santa Fe and Taos and travel to Helltown, with guns and whiskey and tobacco. Comanchero mustangers arrive with their cavallards. Only then will the Comanches go there."

"What do the Comancheros get out of all this trading?"

She moved away from him, to the table, where she gazed at the dancing flame of the candle. True sensed that she didn't relish saying what she was about to say.

"The Comanches bring back many things from a raid. They will trade away horses more suited to the trace than the bit, mules, and sometimes cattle. Many of the things they take from the homes of your people, things they have no use for."

"And captives," said True.

She nodded. "The Comancheros sometimes try on their own to sell them back to their families. Or they are sold into slavery."

"So I've heard. To mines and haciendas down in Mexico. I'll not let that happen to Sadie."

"Don't worry," she said. "If Black Wolf brings your sister to Helltown, we will buy her freedom."

"If?" The alternative was too discouraging to contemplate.

"He may not want to trade her."

"He won't have a choice."

"There are rules all in Helltown must live by. If you go there to kill Black Wolf, you will be killed."

"Who makes these rules?"

"A man named Rodrigo Shay. He is the *patrón*. The Lord of Helltown. He rules with an iron hand. He would not permit you to kill a Comanche warrior who is his guest. This would turn the Comanches away from Helltown forever, and ruin him."

"I don't give a hoot for this Shay feller, or for Helltown. I'm going to get my sister back, no matter what."

An uneasy silence fell like a curtain between them. True felt like a fool standing there tight-lipped and angry, so he went to the bunk, dumped his old saddle on the floor, and sat down. Took the Bowie knife from his belt and commenced to flipping it into the hardpack between his feet.

She sat beside him. He looked at her, and quickly looked away. She was too darn pretty to look at for long. The candlelight touched her dusky skin with a warm amber glow, and caught the auburn highlights in raven-black tendrils of hair falling upon her forehead.

The more he looked the prettier she got, and the prettier she got, the harder it was for him to breathe properly.

"That's quite a knife you have there."

"Not as handsome as yours, ma'am."

She reached under her short brown *chaqueta* and brought out the pearl-handled, fancy-scrolled blade she had put to Gancho's throat. This time True saw the sheath, sewn to the inside of the jacket.

"My father gave this to me. Toledo steel. Made by a famous Spanish metalsmith."

"I was told this here knife was made by a feller named James Black, and is just like the one he made for Jim Bowie. Your father must be well off to afford a knife like that."

"My father is a very powerful man," she said, with a bittersweet smile. "Ruthless, but fair in his own way."

"How'd you come to ride with Comancheros?"

"My father is a Comanchero. I was born on the back of a horse. So I became a mustanger."

"Are you ... Gancho's girl?"

She jumped up, and for a second he thought she was going to tickle his gullet with her Spanish-made toad-sticker.

"He likes to think so. But I am not. So I leave."

"Sorry. Didn't mean to rile you."

The anger bled right out of her. It seemed to him that her anger came like bolts of lightning—quick to strike, quick to fade away.

She touched the corner of her mouth with the tip of her tongue. The way she was looking at him made True uncomfortable.

"I will stay here tonight," she declared.

"What? Here? You can't ... I mean ... it ain't proper."

"I will stay. If I don't, Gancho and his men will try to kill you in the night."

"I can take care of myself."

"Don't be a fool. I won't bite. I will sleep over there."

"On the floor? No, ma'am. That wouldn't be right."

"Right," she echoed, mocking him, a gleam of mischief in her eye. "Proper."

True grimaced. "You can have the dadblasted bunk. I'll take the floor. And that's my final word on the subject."

"*Bueno.* Do what you wish."

True carried his rifle and saddle to the other side of the hut and threw them down. He had the saddle pad and a rolled-up blanket, and figured the gentlemanly thing to do would be to give Sombra the blanket, as the night was turning cold. But he was too put out to think straight. Mad at himself for the most part for acting like a wet-behind-the-ears juniper.

He extinguished the candle and lay down with the pad beneath him and the saddle under his head. Pointed his feet at the door. The hut had no windows, so all he had to worry about was the doorway. He kept his boots on, and the Hawken under his hand.

At first he lay still and scarcely breathing, listening with apprehension to the noise Sombra made as she tossed and turned on the cornhusk mattress. In time, her deep and measured breathing told him that she was asleep.

The darkness was intense. Even when his eyes had fully adjusted, there was nothing to see but a faint bluish border of starlight rimming the door-covering blanket.

Sometime later he rose, blanket in hand, and tried to Indian-up to Sombra. He made less noise than the field mice. He covered her with the blanket, and was about to tiptoe away when he felt her fingers dance with a feather touch across the bony knuckles of his hand. He jumped like a scorched cat.

"Share the blanket with me, True Bowen," she whispered. "It is too cold to sleep on the ground without a cover."

True doubted he would ever feel cold again.

"No, ma'am," he mumbled, and fled across the room, fetching his leg a painful lick on the table corner and tripping over his saddle.

He thought she had gone back to sleep when she spoke once more, in a husky, whispery way that set his ears to burning.

"My name is Sombra, not *ma'am*."

True didn't get much by way of sleep that night.

Twice, as he was about to drift off, he heard the soft and stealthy tread of booted feet out near the corral. One of the Comancheros—maybe Gancho himself—lurking in distant shadow, then fading like a restless spirit into deeper night.

In the palm of that night, during that still and dreamless hour before the first hint of new dawn touches the eastern rim, there was a disturbance in the village.

True heard voices urgently pitched, some cursing, and finally the drumroll of horses at the gallop. Sombra stirred and came awake. True rose, Hawken in hand, hearing a single horse checked sharply in front of the hut. He beat Sombra to the doorway.

"Stay inside," he said.

"Don't tell me what to do."

With a sigh, he swept the blanket aside.

It was Quill Eason. His cinnamon-colored horse was prancing, ready to run. A longrider's dream when it came to horseflesh—deep-chested, long of leg, and high-spirited.

"What's going on?"

White teeth flashed in the nightshadow beneath his wide-brimmed hat, beneath the sweep of mustache.

"We're pulling out, True. Mex cavalry spotted in Zaragosa, and heading this way. I come to warn you. You bein' a Tejano, it would be unhealthy to stay. The Mexicans are still smarting over the way they got roughed up at San Jacinto, you know."

Sombra touched True's arm. "He is right. We should go."

As usual, the idea of running put a sour taste on True's tongue.

"This is Texas, ain't it? They've got no right…"

Eason laughed. "It's plain you don't savvy the way things work down here. Till you get more homesteaders south of the Nueces, this is no man's land. But do what you want."

"The dragoons will kill you," said Sombra.

"Listen to her, Bowen, if you won't listen to me."

"I'll go. Thanks. You're making a habit of looking out for me."

"Let's say you remind me of my brother, and leave it at that."

"You mean Judd."

He went rigid in the saddle. The teeth-flashing grin vanished.

"How did you come by that?"

"I met the man who shot him. Ranger Jack Hule."

"You should take more care with the company you keep, hoss."

True stepped closer to the cinnamon horse. "Why'd you go and kill that banker man in Goliad?"

"He swindled my father, son. Sold him a certificate for land that wasn't his to sell. They took to calling my father a squatter. When they came to drive him off the land, he fought back. He was shot dead. Rutherford didn't pull the trigger, but he might as well have. Took my father's stake and then denied the sale was ever made. After we buried Pa, Judd and I rode into Goliad and set things straight."

"I'm sorry."

"I'm not, except about Judd." Quill shrugged the grief out of his shoulders, and lightened his tone. "Good luck to you both. Maybe we'll meet again, True Bowen, God willing and the creeks don't rise."

He swept the hat off his head and whacked the cinnamon horse on the rump. With a wild coyote yell, he lit out like a man chased by devil dogs. True watched him disappear into the night gloom, narrowing eyes against a swirl of pale dust.

8

Three days they traveled north. Though he wasn't certain of the date, True calculated that, in all probability, he turned twenty on one of those days.

Second day out they ran smack into the first norther of the year. The icy wind whistled in their ears and brought tears to their eyes. Sombra donned a *manga*—a long cloak lined with wolf fur. All True had was a blanket-serape. The wind cut through him. He thought at times that he could feel the blood freezing in his veins. After a day's ride his hands and feet were blocks of ice. He could put them in the flames of their night-camp fire and not feel the burn.

The brasada was altogether different from the fertile land along the Guadalupe. Sand and rock, cactus and chaparral, cut through with hondos so dust-dry it was hard to imagine water had ever flowed in them. So it was for hundreds of miles in every direction, with scarcely a landmark to steer by. A solid gray lid of clouds was firmly set down over the earth, and it was difficult to tell if it was morning or afternoon. There were no stars at night. But all they had to do was turn their faces into the frigid wind to know which way was north.

Sombra sat a lightweight Spanish saddle on an apron-faced sorrel. The saddle was single-cinched, with a sharp cantle and high slim horn, and conchostudded, with a reata tied on either side.

She never seemed to tire, acting like she could ride all month without rest. True was plenty stiff and sore by day's end. He wanted to believe the big difference was the fact that the apron-faced sorrel had the smoothest gait of any horse he had seen, while he bounced across the brush country on the back of the most graceless critter God ever made.

Each night they would camp in a bosky of scrub trees for shelter, and build a strong fire for warmth. Sitting close around the campfire, with the blustery night closing in around them, and the far-off honking of south-flying geese drifting down through the overcast, she spoke for the most part about mustanging. So began True's education on the subject.

Cimarrones usually ran in bands, or *manadas*. The leader was a stallion, the others his mares. The stallion would not tolerate another stallion in the band, but would sometimes permit mules, because mules made excellent lookouts.

There were not enough mares so every stallion could have his own *manada*, and mareless stallions sometimes grouped together. Bands of these outcasts would scatter when chased. But a *manada* with a stallion would run together unless the stallion was killed. Then the mares would scatter. So it was not usually a good idea to kill the stallion.

However, every *manada* had its own range, its *querencia*, in most cases not more than twenty miles square. A chased *manada* would sooner or later circle, rather than leave its range.

And the band always watered at the same place every day, unless chased away. At the same time every day. If wild horses drank at a particular place along a river, they would travel miles along that river, without once stopping to drink, until they reached their favorite place.

The mustang was a creature of the open plains. It would not go into woods, or through a canyon, except to get to water or to escape capture. It was not at all like the black cattle, which hid in the brush like wanted men when hunted. The mustang used speed and endurance, rather than guile, to remain free.

The techniques used to catch them allowed for this. Indeed, the most common one was to run them, using relays of riders. This took days. Eventually the weaker colts and mares dropped out of the band. A stallion who was a good *manadero* did not always run ahead of his mares. Sometimes he dropped back to drive them on. Sometimes he forced a mare to leave her faltering colt behind. And every now and then a stallion would kill a colt to save the mare from capture.

"The most important thing to remember about a wild stallion," Sombra told him, "is that when you put a rope on him, he will turn on you, and do his best to kill you."

At dawn of the third day, as they were about to break camp, huddling for one more precious minute of warmth around their fire, a distant blood-curdling howl floated on the damp, white morning fog.

Sombra leaped to her feet and ran for her already-saddled horse, in a hushed and excited tone of voice urging True to hurry along. He kicked out the fire and climbed aboard King George, and they rode cautiously to the rim of the bosky and gazed out across the fog-wreathed flat.

Another howl broke the morning stillness, followed by a series of grunting barks, and then the shrill whinny of a horse, the thunder of hooves.

"What…?" began True.

She gestured sharply, which he took to mean that he was to keep his big mouth shut.

The thunder grew louder. King George started fidgeting, and True leaned forward to lay a hand over the mule's nostrils. This gesture usually had a calming effect on the knobhead, and kept him from braying.

Suddenly the fog lifted a few feet off the ground, and True got his first eyeful of wild mustangs.

They were coming straight at the thicket at a dead run, chased by a pack of wolves.

Twenty in number, blacks and browns and duns, they galloped toward the bosky in a tight cluster. King George went crazy at the sight of them, braying and bucking so abruptly that True was caught off-guard, and thrown.

Mad as a hornet, he bounced up and socked the ornery hardtail in the jawbone. King George settled down some then, trembling and glassy-eyed.

The commotion turned the mockeys away from the thicket, about a hundred feet shy. Seeing their chance, the wolves cut them off. Surrounded, the mustangs milled, then sorted themselves out and formed a circle. They stood their ground, facing out. In this way they presented a barricade of snapping teeth and slashing hooves.

Then True saw the white stallion.

He had been running behind the *manada* before, fighting a rear-guard action against the pack and driving his mares on. Now he circled the band, nipping at a mare to keep her in tight formation, then turning to confront a wolf darting in too close.

"It cannot be!" gasped Sombra. "The White Pacer!"

No question, thought True, the white was one magnificent horse. Even he, no expert on the subject of cayuses, knew that much at a glance. White as snow from muzzle to tail, except for ears of ebony black. His mane hung long and thick on both sides of his neck. Noticeably larger than the other mustangs, he was a proud and fierce creature.

True couldn't tell for certain how many wolves were in the pack. All he saw, for the most part, were darting gray streaks in the stunted chaparral. One got so bold as to go for the stallion's back legs. The white whirled, caught the lobo by the neck with his teeth and flung the yelping wolf twenty feet. Quick as thought, the stallion lunged forward and stamped the lobo to death.

Seeing this, the other wolves gave up the fight. They began to slink away through the brush. The stallion chased one a short distance before returning to his mares. With a shrill whinny, he reared and pawed the air. The mares broke the circle and started to gallop away from the bosky.

"I must have him!" cried Sombra, and before True could say a word in warning, she had kicked the sorrel into a standing-start gallop, bursting out of the thicket with one of her reatas in hand.

It seemed to True that the white stallion was trouble. What he could do to a big lobo he could surely do to a slip of a girl.

True tried to get into the saddle and go after her, but King George was dancing around and pulling back and in general trying to shake him loose. The mule had gone plumb wild, wanting to take up with the mockeys. True had all he could handle just holding onto rein leather.

A horse screamed. True looked around in time to see the reata loop settle neatly over the stallion's head. Sombra had caught him by surprise. He still had wolves on his mind, and the smell of the dead lobo's blood was strong in his nostrils.

When he felt the rope on his neck the stallion went berserk. Sombra dallied the reata around the biscuit of her saddle, and when the stallion hit the end of the line, True thought the sorrel was going to be pulled clean off its feet.

The stallion twisted in the air. He came down kicking, then reared, biting at the rope. Sombra's sorrel locked its front legs and lowered its back end, anchoring down for dear life.

Sombra was shaking her second reata into a loop when the stallion charged.

"Look out!" yelled True.

The stallion plowed into the sorrel. Sombra fell with her horse. Entangled in the sorrel's flailing legs, the stallion came crashing down as well. When the great horse rose, the neck loop had loosened, and he shook out of it as neat as could be.

True figured the stallion would turn and run. But as Sombra stood, swinging the second reata over her head, the white spun, snorting, and charged again.

Sombra backed away from this onslaught and collided with the sorrel as it struggled upright. She fell, and the sorrel tied it on with the white stallion.

They met on hind legs, screaming the most ungodly sounds True had ever heard, and hurled themselves against one another, raking with front hooves, ears laid back, teeth bared. They pivoted and kicked with hind legs, spun and lunged for each other's jugular. It was a fierce, thrashing whirlwind of violence.

And Sombra was right in the middle of it.

True climbed the reins, trying to get closer to King George, and cursing a blue streak. The Hawken was cradled in two saddle strings tied in loops. He got hold of the stock and pulled the rifle free. King George yanked back so hard that True lost his one-handed grip on the reins. The mule whirled, gave one good high kick that True dodged easily, as he had expected a parting shot.

The Hawken was loaded, with a cap under the hammer. He wasn't certain the load was still tamped down tight, with all the mule's acrobatics, so he pulled the ramrod and made sure as he ran out into the open, yelling up a storm. The fighting horses paid him no mind. True stopped, aimed at the white stallion, and fired.

He missed.

Still hollering at the top of his lungs, he reloaded as he ran. He had to get closer for a sure shot. The horses were spinning around in a cloud of dust, faster than tail-chasing dogs.

But True never got a second shot off. The stallion broke away from the sorrel and took off at a high-stepping pace which covered ground faster than a full-out gallop.

Sombra was unharmed. True helped her up. She looked after the white stallion, rueful and starry-eyed, in time to see the horse vanish like a wraith in fog. Then she looked at True, and laughed.

"What's so all-fired funny?" he snapped. "You could've been killed."

"I laugh at myself. I lost my head when I saw the White Pacer. I made a foolish mistake. I should have thrown the first loop at his forefeet. But I had to get closer for that, and I couldn't wait."

"Well, our ox is in a ditch now. My blockhead mule lit out, and I don't see hide nor hair of your horse."

"Don't be angry with me," she pleaded, with a gentle smile.

She whistled and the sorrel whinnied, came trotting meekly out of the fog and straight to her. His neck and withers were gashed.

"King George won't be that easy to catch," promised True. "He don't answer to whistles, or anything short of an ax handle between the eyes."

"You may never catch him. He has taken up with the maroons. The white stallion will probably kill him."

That was depressing news. True had become more attached to the mean-spirited hardtail than he had realized.

"What's so damn special about the white stallion, anyhow?" he asked as he climbed up on the sorrel.

They had to ride double, and there wasn't enough room in the tight-fitting Spanish saddle for them both, so he straddled the sorrel's croup, clinging with both hands to the cantle.

"Didn't you see him? He is a legend. He is one of a kind. His only gait out of the walk is a pace. He never breaks into a gallop. He does not need to. Within a mile he will outdistance every other horse."

She went on to tell him that many had tried to capture the white. No ordinary *cimarrone*, he would leave his range and find another if pursued too hotly. This was something no other stallion would do. Mustangers had tried every trick, without success. Some had even tried creasing him. The white had been shot, more than once, according to the legend. He knew the sound of the rifle. It was Sombra's opinion that this was why the white broke and ran after True fired his first shot.

"You mean to say he knew I was fixin' to kill him?"

"That would have been a terrible waste. He is worth a hundred ordinary mustangs. For the white stallion, Black Wolf would gladly trade your sister. The white is big medicine among the Comanche."

They traveled another mile before True spoke again.

"Reckon maybe I ought to try and catch him, then."

"Don't try. I don't think he will be taken alive."

"But you tried to."

"I should have known better. At least now I can say I put a rope on him. That, in itself, is an accomplishment."

The next morning they came to a brawling creek and turned west along it. The clouds opened up and sleet began to slant against them, stinging the skin. Now, on top of cold, they were wet. Hunching their bodies against the driving downpour, they pushed on, their breath steaming.

An hour later they forded the rocky creek and came to a small stone house backed up against a steep shale bluff. Chimney smoke drifted low across the little clearing and into the trees where they paused. Carried on it was the spicy aroma of cooking, and True's stomach started growling.

He heard a rumbling voice raised in song. Being tone-deaf, he could hardly make out one tune from another, but he recognized the words.

"Rock of Ages, cleft for me,
Let me hide myself in thee. ..."

As they drew closer to the house, the singing stopped, and a man filled the doorway.

He was big, his shoulders brushing the doorframe. He had to stoop to come through. His head was bald as a baby's behind. A Negro, he wore buckskin leggins and beaded moccasins and a hickory shirt with the sleeves torn out. True doubted that arms the size of this man's would fit into sleeves.

A small gold ring dangled from the black man's ear. Angling down his forehead was a scar, crossing the bridge of his nose and his right cheek to the jawbone, giving him a fearsome demeanor.

Here was a man, mused True, who could literally tear a person limb from limb and not raise a sweat in the doing of it.

"Sombra," he muttered, "we'd best get out of here."

"Don't be silly. This is our home for the winter."

Home? True took a quick look at the house, a lean-to and a picket corral. Then he turned a wary eye back to the Goliath in the doorway.

Sombra slipped off the saddle, ground-hitched the sorrel, and walked right up to the big man.

"Cómo está, Golden?"

The fierce, scowling face broke into a grin.

"Sombra!"

He lunged forward with arms thrown wide, snatched her off her feet in a swirling embrace, then set her down and held her at arm's length.

"Let me get a look at you, child! The Lord be praised!" His voice boomed like the crack of thunder. "Yore a sight for sore eyes, girl."

True got off the sorrel and stood well apart, not wishing to interfere in this happy reunion.

Golden glanced at him. "Who's this hombre?"

"Golden, this is True Bowen. He and I are going to catch wild horses. Will you help us?"

"You still with Gancho?"

"No."

"Glad to hear it. Mighty glad. You know I'll help. I'll do anything for you, child. Now you come on inside out of this weather. You'll catch your death, you ain't more careful. I gots hoe cake and son-of-a-gun stew ready to be et. Killed a wild *ladino* that tried to sharpen his horns on my rib cage. True Bowen, throw that red horse into the lean-to and haul the tack on in the house. *Mi casa es su casa.*"

A shaggy zebra dun occupied the lean-to. Removing saddle, pad, and bridle, True tied the sorrel alongside the dun, found an empty gunnysack, and used this to rub the sorrel down and dry him off. Then he hauled the gear to the rock house.

The place was built to last. The walls were two feet thick. The floor was smooth stone. Viga roof poles supported a ply of pickets, on which rested a thick layer of sod squares. Not a drop of rain leaked through. An inner wall of rawhide-lashed pickets cut the house into two rooms. The connecting doorway was draped with an old brown blanket. There were two front windows, one in either room, with heavy oak-plank shutters, and a narrow door in the rear wall.

A fine fire blazed in the hearth, and the house was plenty warm. Golden and Sombra sat at a split-log table, plates before them, a pot of stew and a platter of hoe cake near at hand.

"Let the gear drop and set," said Golden.

True didn't need to be told twice. He was hungry enough to eat a horned toad backwards. He sat where a third wooden plate had been placed, and promptly made a boarding-house reach for the hoe cake.

Golden lashed out and grabbed his wrist in a bone-grinding grip.

"Boy, where's your manners?"

"Manners?" echoed True, bewildered.

"We may be out in the middle of the frontier, but that's no reason to act uncivilized. Under this roof, the custom is to say grace over a meal. Since you're the guest, I reckon we'll let you do the honors."

"Me?" True looked to Sombra for help, but she just smiled. Then he looked at Golden, who was stern-faced. Finally he looked at the big leather-bound well-worn Bible on the table next to Golden's massive arm.

Feeling self-conscious, he dipped his head a little, and waited until they had bowed theirs and weren't watching him anymore.

"Bless the meat and damn the skin; throw back your ears and all pitch in."

He looked up into a fierce scowl from Golden.

"Amen," said Sombra, and burst out laughing.

A smile tugged at the corners of Golden's mouth.

"You heathens," he said. "Dig in."

9

Born a slave on a plantation in the Louisiana delta country, Golden one day snapped the neck of a sadistic overseer whose whip he had felt one too many times. Fleeing into the swamp, he had fallen in with the pirate crowd of Jean Lafitte.

Lafitte was making a profitable career out of waylaying Spanish cargo ships and selling the stolen goods in New Orleans. The United States and Spain were at peace, so Lafitte had to smuggle the booty in as contraband. The goods were sold to black-marketeers at meeting places deep in the swamp.

Golden was there when Lafitte offered his services to Andrew Jackson after war broke out between the United States and Great Britain, and he fought alongside Lafitte when the pirates helped Old Hickory whup the British at the Battle of New Orleans.

After Lafitte's death, Golden turned his back on the sea and entered Mexico. Trouble with authorities drove him north into the desert frontier of Coahuila. There he had taken up with Gancho.

"His real name is José Muñoz," said Golden. "He used to be a sergeant in the regular Mexican army. He was accused of knowing, in the Biblical way, the wife of the *comandante*. Way I heard it, many men knew the general's wife. She was a real Jezebel. But she grew careless, and contracted a disease which she couldn't keep secret from her husband. She pointed the finger at Muñoz.

"The entire regiment was assembled to see Sergeant Muñoz get a hundred lashes. Muñoz was court-martialed, and sentenced to life in prison. While he was there he stole food, and the guards cut off his hand in punishment. Working with the prison smithy, Muñoz forged himself an iron hook on a wooden cup which strapped onto his arm. Men took to calling him Gancho—Hook—after that.

"He spent a couple years in prison, and then escaped. One night he paid that general's wife a visit, as she lay sleeping in her bed. He took her, then cut her throat. Before dying she let out a scream that brought the sentries running. Gancho killed all but one. That one claimed Gancho fought like a crazy man. I reckon he was. He's been loco all the time I've known him. But he got away, disappeared into the desert, and took to leading a pack of Comanchero wranglers. It got too crazy for these old bones after a while so I headed out.

"Bowen, I've killed more men than I care to count," Golden said regretfully. "I've committed a heap of sin. But I never killed except in self-defense, and I never stole from the poor. Same can't be said for Gancho.

"Didn't much care for his mustanging ways, either. Awful cruel. There's ways to break a wild horse without half-killin' the poor critter. But Gancho and his men didn't care. They'd shoot mares to capture colts. Then they'd tie a hair rope to the colt's tail and one of its front legs, so the colt couldn't run. The colt couldn't walk a mile before the inside of its thighs were rubbed bloody raw.

"Another little trick they used was cutting a mustang's knee ligament open and letting out all the joint water. After that, one man could handle forty-fifty crippled horses all by himself. They'd never run again, of course, but they could still breed and make colts."

Golden frowned at these dark memories. "I seen the same thing done to a slave, Bowen. After a while I'd had a gutful of Gancho and his ways. Come out here to live in peace. I've done a lot of bad things in my life. Don't intend to do more. The Lord'll have to be in a mighty forgiving mood when I go to stand before Him in final judgment."

True reckoned this was why Golden pitched in so wholeheartedly to help get Sadie back from the Comanches. He had no stake in such a dangerous enterprise, except that, on account of all the bad he had done, he was hoping to balance the scales a little by doing something good for somebody.

Several days after their arrival at the rock house, the norther blew on by. The skies cleared, and the wind turned southerly and gentle. Sunny days became pleasantly cool, though the nights remained bitterly cold.

Sombra and Golden set out one morning to find something for True to ride, as he would be poor help in the catching of mustangs on foot.

They were gone for the better part of a week. True did not much care for being left behind, and was down on himself for losing King George. There wasn't a lot for him to do around the rock house, so he spent most of the time wandering. He always carried the Hawken. Sometimes he would also take an ax, and cut bundles of firewood he'd carry back to the house. He bagged a whitetail deer, which he dressed out, smoking strips of venison over an open fire and staking the skin out on a hoop of supple willow branches.

One morning his aimless foray took him up-creek about two miles from the rock house. There he discovered a deep clear pool of water, which looked to be spring-fed. Though the water was cold, and the day cool, he couldn't resist shedding his clothes and taking a swim. He came out shivering but refreshed, and no longer host to a pound of dirt and a passel of gray backs.

He was pulling on his trousers when he heard horses.

His first thought was Comanches. He grabbed the rest of his clothes and his rifle and ducked down in the rocks, out of sight.

Wasn't Comanche, though. It was the white stallion and his *manada.*

The white was in the lead this time, as the band came through the shedding trees to the rim of the pool directly across from True's place of concealment. The mares paused as the stallion paced this way and that a moment, sniffing the air and looking warily about.

True was downwind and well hidden. He saw no sign of King George, and figured the mule for dead.

The stallion whickered. At the signal, the mares began to drink. White Pacer drank last, and was last to leave when the band returned to the trees.

All the way back to the rock house, True couldn't get what Sombra had said out of his mind. About how the white stallion was big medicine among the Comanche, and how Black Wolf would gladly give Sadie up to have him.

Golden and Sombra came back the day after, towing a sidelined bay stallion. They put him in the high-sided corral, still hobbled forefeet to hind.

"Came up on a bunch of outcasts," explained Golden, as True peered curiously through two of the upright pickets that formed the sides of the corral. "Naturally they split up. This feller was the best-looking of the lot, but we never would've caught him 'cept I managed to haze him into a stand of cholla before he started pulling away. That slowed him down enough for Sombra to catch him. Cholla can really lame a horse, Bowen, but it ain't permanent."

Having seen the white stallion again, True was unimpressed by the bay. He told of sighting White Pacer at the spring.

Golden frowned. "Sombra mentioned your run-in with the white. He moved into this neck of the woods last spring. But you can just put him out of your mind. No point wastin' time trying to catch him. Likely get yourself killed, were you to try. He's a devil horse, and best left alone. Now, we've gots to break this wild 'un here. Or I should say *you* gots to. So let's get on with the business at hand."

"I don't know the first thing about horse-breaking," confessed True. "I was a farmer—"

"No time like the present to learn."

The first couple days they kept the bay tied up short to the snubbing post. Every time True brought him a *morral* of wild oats and mesquite beans or a bucket of water, the horse would try to kick or bite him. True rebuked him in a stern tone of voice and left the ungrateful wretch to go without for half a day before trying again.

On the third day the horse accepted the offerings. On the fourth he licked salt from True's hand.

The next step was to put Golden's saddle on him, loose-cinched. They left the hull on him all one day and through the following night. In the morning they tied bundles of firewood to either side of the saddle. This was to get the horse used to wearing a saddle with weight on it.

The day after that, it was time for True to get into the saddle.

Golden blindfolded the bay. The horse stood stock-still as True climbed aboard. In addition to the saddle cinch, a strong rope was tied around the animal's barrel. True stuck his knees under it and held onto it with one hand, clutching the reins with the other.

When Golden removed the blindfold the bay lunged at the sky and landed with its legs locked and back kinked. True sailed across the corral and lay a moment where he fell, the world spinning.

Golden leaned over him and smiled.

"He's gonna be a real kidney-buster, Bowen."

"We'll see," wheezed True, trying to get his wind.

He mounted the bay again. This time he stayed on ten seconds longer. The bay reared, pitched, slammed into the side of the corral, and as a last resort rolled over, crushing True into the hardpack.

Golden helped him up and held on until True found his legs.

"He's got fire in his belly, Bowen. Do you?"

True spat a mouthful of dust and shook loose.

Sombra had the bay roped and snubbed, and it stood stiff and trembling, four-legged fury waiting to explode. True's bacon was burned now. He twisted the animal's ear, hard as he was able, until he had settled in the saddle. Golden pulled the loop off and they went at it again.

The bay kicked, pitched, bucked, leaped, twisted, reared, and everything in between, but True held on. Gradually the bay tired and some of the violence went out of him, and True was beginning to think he had won when Golden threw the corral gate open.

With a screaming whinny, the bay saw freedom and shot out of the corral like a bullet out of a barrel. True sawed on the reins, but could not slow the horse. The bay was pure streaked lightning. The speed took True's breath away. He clamped his legs around the mustang's heaving barrel and held on for dear life.

The wind in his teeth, the bay made straight for the creek and plunged in. There he stood, rigid as a fencepost, for several minutes. True dared not move an inch.

With a snort, the horse lunged to the bank and galloped a good mile downstream, leaping over deadfall, twisting through the trees, and making sure to run under every low-hanging limb along the way. Branches tore at True's clothes and hair and slashed at his face. But he stuck to that horse like a wet blanket.

Tuckered out, the bay slowed to a canter, then a walk, and finally stopped altogether. He began to crop at sparse brown grass. True risked trying to turn him with the reins. The bay snapped at the bit and whirled. True tapped his heels, and they started back in the direction of the rock house at a high lope.

His legs ached, his bones hurt, his face and neck were gashed in a dozen places, but True was grinning like a fool.

He named the bay Lightning and the two became a team. True would spend hours riding by himself, fighting off the hollow feeling of homesickness and dejection. One such time, he'd been out all day and night slipped up on him. As darkness gathered among the skeletons of the nearby creek-bottom trees, he was rousing himself to return to the rock house when he heard a rider coming.

It was Sombra. Her sorrel's blaze showed like a white flag in the gloom. At first True was annoyed by her intrusion. But as she dismounted and stepped close, her beauty made his anger fade.

"I was fixin' to come back," he said. "You needn't have come looking for me."

"I wanted to be with you. To give you something."

"I ain't got nothing to give in return."

"Yes, you have."

She slipped her arms around his neck, and pressed her body against his. A smoldering fire in her eyes and in her touch set his body aflame. Her lips brushed his, light as a feather, and he folded her in his arms and held her tight, burying his face in that long, fragrant raven hair hanging loose about her shoulders. A warm contentment surged through him, and a new strength.

They stood there in that embrace for a long time. Night closed in around them. The nearby creek sang its endless lilting song. Neither of them wanted to let go.

Eventually they rode back to the rock house. Not a word passed between them. There was no need for words.

They got back to find Golden hunkered down by the fireplace. Sombra went directly to the other room. In the past she had slept there, while the two men nighted on buffalo robes laid out on the floor by the fire. True now noticed his bedding was missing.

"What's the matter with you?" asked Golden, poking new life into the dying fire with a stick.

"Nothin'." Tugging on his ear, True tried to figure out what was going on.

"We'll be leaving early in the morning. Got maroons to catch. So you'd best turn in."

True just stood there. Golden looked up at him, deadly serious.

"Sombra's like a daughter to me, Bowen. I'll expect you to do right by her, you hear? She got strong feelings for you, son."

True was too tongue-tied to even attempt explaining his intentions to Golden. So he simply nodded.

Golden gazed into the fire.

"Bowen, there's something I want you to know. In the back of my Bible, on the flyleaf, is a map I've drawn. Shows how to get from here to Helltown."

True glanced at the leather-bound book on the table.

"We're all going together, aren't we, Golden?"

"You never know what the morrow holds in store. Should anything happen to me or, God forbid, Sombra, you'll be able to find Helltown on your own with that map."

"Thank you."

The big man nodded, and did not look away from the fire.

"G'night, True."

True went through the blanketed doorway, as dazed as the first time Lightning had thrown him.

Sombra lay on the narrow bed, a buffalo robe pulled up so that only the dusky curve of a bare shoulder was visible in the flickering firelight slipping through the pickets from the other room. Lose tendrils of hair fell across her face.

True shucked his clothes, and she lifted the robe. He wasn't the least bit embarrassed as he slid in beside her.

This was where he was meant to be.

10

Three days ride from the rock house, they found a *charco*, a pool of water, in an otherwise bone-dry wash, at the base of a steep bluff. There was plenty of scrub timber near at hand. Golden looked the spot over judiciously, and finally gave it the nod.

"We'll build the corral here."

True saw no sign of wild horses having watered at the pool, and so remarked.

"Don't fret about that, Bowen. Sombra's goin' to bring the maroons to us."

"How?"

"You'll see."

They had brought axes and cane knives, and set to chopping down the live oak and blackjack. First they built a lean-to, a hundred yards from the pool, the open side facing south, a thicket of granjero on the north side for a windbreak. The structure was plenty large enough to accommodate all three of them, plus their gear. It would be their home for the next several weeks.

Once the lean-to was finished, they started on the corral. Its south side was the bluff. The other three sides were made of brush packed down tightly between pairs of deeply planted posts set a few feet apart and lashed together with rawhide. From the corral opening on the north side they fashioned "wings," flaring rows of deadwood. These did not need to be high or impenetrable. Running mustangs would crowd together to keep away from the wings, and thus would be funneled through the opening and into the corral. Once the horses were in the corral, the opening could be blocked with a long pole lashed into place, to which upright pickets were tied.

The corral was circular, and about a hundred feet in diameter. It enclosed the pool at the base of the bluff.

With the corral done, they struck out due west. Within a day they were on the trail of a *manada.* Before dusk they sighted it. Golden carried a telescope, which he claimed had been given to him by Jean Lafitte. Sitting their horses on a rocky bench, they shared the glass to get a close look at twenty-five wild horses a quarter-mile away, in the valley below. The mockeys grazed quietly beneath a darkening sky striped with gold-rimmed purple clouds.

That night they camped on the high and windswept bench, without a fire. True had a hard time surrendering to sleep. The sense that something important was on the verge of happening kept him wound tighter than an eight-day clock. He listened for hours to distant coyote sing-alongs. The eastern sky was pearling with the new dawn before he finally drifted off.

He woke to find Golden putting Sombra's Spanish rig on Lightning. Sombra swung up onto the bare back of her blaze-faced sorrel. Until now True had been the one to ride bareback, as they were short one saddle.

"You ready, child?" asked Golden.

"I am ready," she said, her eyes bright with excitement.

"*Vaya con Dios.*"

"Hold on a doggone minute," said True, hurrying up. "What's going on here?"

She reached down to touch his face.

"I would not have left without saying goodbye, True."

"Goodbye? Where are you going?"

"Down there. Alone. If they accept me, I will join that *manada.* I'll be among the maroons for days, perhaps weeks. You and Golden will trail behind. In time, if all goes well, I will bring them to the corral."

"If they *accept* you? How can that happen? It doesn't make sense."

"Watch and learn, boy." Golden smiled. "Watch and learn."

Sombra kicked the sorrel into a canter, and headed for that distant bunch of mustangs.

At first the *manada* ran from her. She did not give chase. She never put the sorrel into a run, following instead in their wake. When she came into view again, the mustangs would run as before, leaving her far behind. She kept plodding along after.

She dogged them in this way for one whole day and part of the next. True and Golden followed, keeping their distance. So far back that, most of the time, True needed Golden's pirate eyeglass to see her.

Eventually the mustangs ceased to run at Sombra's approach. She wasn't acting as though she wanted to catch them, to rob them of their freedom, to harm them in any way. They no longer equated her scent with danger. When they stopped to graze, she stopped. When they moved, she moved. The wild horses became more curious than afraid. But when the *manadero*, the stallion, came too close, Sombra would turn the sorrel away. She never permitted the stallion to get near.

Three days out it became obvious that Sombra and the sorrel were traveling with the *manada*, not following it.

"So far so good," said Golden. "Now she gots to get them to follow her lead."

From then on, every other day or so, True and Golden would ride close. The mustangs would flee. So would Sombra. The third time this happened, Sombra and the sorrel actually rounded up the *manada* and directed the flight.

Every few days, True and Golden would circle ahead of the band and leave a pouch of venison jerky hanging from a conspicuous tree, Sombra's red sash tied to it. By dint of long observation, they now had a good idea as to the boundaries of this group's *querencia*, and the ways in which the *manada* traveled its range. Sombra never failed to find and take the pouch, leaving the sash for use the next time.

The days turned into a week, then two weeks. The weather held until the end of the second week, when True woke one morning to find the brasada blanketed by four inches of new snow. The emptied clouds came apart and drifted away, and the sun shone on a world as pretty as he had ever seen it.

"This is good," said Golden. "Soon she should try to move them to the corral."

True wholeheartedly agreed. Though he could always borrow the telescope and see her—which he often did—he was missing Sombra something fierce. He wanted to hold her in his arms again.

Little by little, mare by mare, Sombra took the allegiance of the band away from the stallion. Had this threat to his mastery come from the blazed sorrel alone, the stallion would have known how to deal with the problem. But it wasn't just another male horse—it was Sombra *and* the sorrel. Not stallion or mare, gelding or jack, but a new and different kind of creature. The *manadero* could not fight it or outsmart it, and so was powerless to stop the subtle erosion of his control.

The mares began to look to Sombra and the sorrel for leadership. She and her horse demonstrated all the traits of a good *manadero*. They were wary coming upon the day-old tracks of a wolf pack. They led the flight from the fresh-killed carcass of a whitetail doe fallen prey, by the sign, to a panther. They shied away from any snakelike branch half-hidden in the grass, any peculiarly shaped bush. When they led the way to the *manada*'s favorite watering spot, they smelled for danger, kept alert, and drank last.

Well into the third week, after another good snow, Golden led True off the trail of the band for the first time. He could tell True was upset about leaving Sombra.

"We'll be back with her in a day or two, Bowen. Time we put the finishing touches to this work of art."

They tracked and killed the panther which had slain the whitetail, took the big cat's carcass to the favorite watering spot, and went off a ways to settle in and watch.

The next time the *manada* came to drink, the blood smell of the dead panther drove them away, all in a frenzy. As was by now her duty, Sombra led the stampede on her blaze-faced sorrel.

She then took them straight to the *charco* at the base of the bluff.

The recent snow disguised the corral, making it look like just another feature in the rough landscape. The mustangs trooped right down the wings and through the opening. Only the stallion balked. That wily old son knew something was up. He sounded the alarm, but the mares no longer gave heed. The stallion dusted out on his own, and they let him go without a quarrel, closing the gate on twenty-four wild maroons.

Sombra was exhausted. For three weeks she had lived on the sorrel's back, with precious little to eat or drink, and in the bitter heart of winter. True had to carry her to the lean-to. Slender to begin with, she was terribly ganted now. He bundled her up in a buffalo robe, next to a strong fire, and got some hot grub into her.

More than ever before, he was filled with love for her. So much love that he couldn't, try as he might, find the words to adequately express his feelings. But she saw it in his eyes, and laid the sweetest smile he had ever seen upon him.

When she fell asleep, he went to the corral. Golden had climbed one of the pole-and-brush walls to observe the *manada*. True clambered up there alongside.

"Rough-lookin' bunch of critters, aren't they?" remarked Golden.

They were small and wiry, shaggy with their winter coats. Not thoroughbreds, certainly, but to True they were the finest bunch of horses he had ever laid eyes on, because they were the key to Sadie's rescue.

"They're just like the Comanch' like 'em," added Golden. "I reckon they'll do to see your sister free."

"Sombra did all this for me," murmured True. "What can I ever do to repay her?"

Golden laid a hand on his shoulder.

"Just love her, True. That's all she wants."

He knew he always would.

They left the blaze-faced sorrel in the corral with the wild horses for several days, while Sombra recuperated. Then they struck out for the rock house. True half-expected the mockeys to bolt once free of the corral; instead, they placidly followed Sombra and the sorrel. True hung back with Golden, downwind and out of sight.

Three days later they were home, the mustangs tucked away in the picket corral.

"We'll bring 'em out one at a time, and at least have 'em cavvy-broke before we head for Helltown," said Golden as they sat, first night back, around the fireplace.

True remembered his bone-bruising experience with Lightning, and Golden chuckled at the expression on his face.

"We won't break 'em to the saddle, Bowen. After all, these maroons are for the Comanch'. No, we just want to be able to handle them during our trip."

"When do we leave?"

"Few weeks. At first sign of green-up."

Golden's way of taming mustangs was a technique used by Indians. It was not excessively brutal, as were so many *mesteñero* methods.

The mockeys were lassoed and brought out singly. While True and Sombra held the plunging mare in place with their reatas, Golden approached the horse slowly, uttering soft grunting noises from deep in his chest, and making peculiar, graceful motions with his arms that captivated the mare. The horse soon stopped fighting against the reatas.

Golden then placed a ghost cord on the mare—a long string tied around the animal's lower jaw, over the tongue. The reatas were removed. The ghost cord was all Golden needed to exercise control over the mare. Tightened, it pressured sensitive areas and subdued the horse.

Next, Golden ran his hands over the mare, horse-talking constantly. This went on for hours. The mockey came to realize there was nothing to fear from the scent or touch of man. Then came the blanket, passed slowly in front of the mare's eyes, and gently over her back. If the horse acted up, Golden tightened the ghost cord.

The last step was to saddle their own mounts and ride out with the mare in tow, led with the ghost cord. This got the mustang accustomed to the idea of traveling in the company of a person on horseback.

In time they took three or four of the half-tamed maroons out with them. If one broke and ran, Sombra gave chase and brought it down with the *mangana*, the forefoot lasso. After two or three such falls, even the most recalcitrant mare realized life wasn't so bad with the herd, after all.

Eventually they were able to take the whole bunch out for a day of grazing, without a single maroon giving trouble. They couldn't be ridden, but they were cavvy-broke, and could be driven.

True was in high spirits. The worst, he thought, was over. All they had to do was get these horses to Helltown, trade them for Sadie's release, and then …

Then what?

Once Sadie was free, what would he do? Take her back to the Guadalupe River valley, where together they could rebuild the Bowen cabin and sow new crops in the Bowen fields?

He came to realize he didn't have any desire to return to farming. This wild, free life out here in the untamed brasada was in his blood now. What he really wanted, once Sadie was free, was to live here with Sombra. Perhaps they could catch wild horses for a living.

Sombra was also wondering what the future held in store.

One uncommonly warm February day, she and True took a walk along the creek, straying further from the house than intended. They ended up at the spring-fed hole, sat on the big, flat-topped boulder. True put his arm around her, and she rested her head on his shoulder. For the longest time they took in the remote beauty around them and savored the rich contentment of being together.

She asked him what he intended to do after Sadie's rescue.

"I'll take her to see our brother Chance, and then I want to come back here. I want to stay here with you, Sombra."

It was coming on dark before they got back to the rock house. They were so wrapped up in each other they got in too close before noticing the blood bay tied to a chunk of wood at the side of the place. Neither of them had ever seen that horse before.

The door swung open. A big man stood silhouetted against the golden glow of firelight. His face was hidden in deep shadow. As he performed a mocking bow and sweeping gesture for them to enter, he turned his body slightly, and True recognized the craggy features, the gun-barrel eyes beneath jutting brows.

"Well, if it ain't the game rooster himself," said Ranger Hule. He spat a brown stream of tobacco juice. "Fancy meeting you here."

Two men suddenly appeared around the corner of the house. Both held pistols.

One of them was Chance.

He almost dropped his teeth when he saw True, and by reflex lowered his gun.

"Keep 'em covered!" rasped Hule.

"This here's my brother, Sergeant."

"I know who the hell he is. But as you can see, he's riding with Comancheros now. That makes him the enemy, Ranger Bowen."

Chance brought the gun back up, his features turning hard and cold.

11

"**Y**ou'd be wise to drop that long rifle," said Hule.

True dropped the Hawken.

"What the hell are you doing here, True?" asked Chance.

"I live here."

Chance's eyes flicked with disfavor to Sombra. "With a nigger and a Mex whore?"

True balled up his fists. His voice shook with anger.

"Better watch your mouth, or I'll knock your teeth out."

The man next to Chance, the one True didn't know, chuckled. "There's some hard bark on this young sapling."

"I reckon that's so," nodded Hule. "He took a Yamparika lance through the middle and he's still above snakes. Call the boys in, Lon."

Lon put two fingers in his mouth and let go with a shrill whistle.

Thirty riders came out of the twilight gloom gathering beneath the creek-bottom trees. They walked their mounts across the clearing, checked them in front of the rock house. Hard lean men, most of them bearded, wearing trail-grimed buckskin or homespun, and bristling with weapons. Tight-lipped, steel-eyed hombres.

Texas Rangers.

"You men step down," said Hule. "Breathe those ponies, and roll a smoke." He looked at True. "You and your sweetheart best come inside."

He led the way. Chance entered last, shutting the door.

Golden sat at the split-log table, with Captain Ben Steelman across from him. Steelman was pointing his gun at Golden. He

76

wasn't looking at Golden, though, but rather at Golden's Bible, which he was idly leafing through.

There was blood on Golden's temple, and it was dripping down the side of his face and onto his neck.

"You all right?" asked True.

"I'll live. One of these gentlemen snuck up on me whilst I was out fetchin' in some firewood."

"I did," said Hule, sounding proud. "Can't say I'm sorry."

"You are," said True.

Hule snorted. "You've got a big mouth."

True didn't respond.

Steelman's gaze rose from the Good Book and fastened bleakly on True.

"Private Bowen, isn't this boy kin to you?"

"My brother," replied Chance, like it pained him to admit it.

Steelman tugged thoughtfully on his iron gray goatee, flinty eyes looking True over. True felt like a dead man being measured for a pine box by the undertaker.

"Boy," said Steelman, "this is the last place you want to be."

"It's where I am."

"Get over by the fireplace. You too, ma'am."

They did as he bade them. This put them behind Golden, and farther from the front door. Sombra put a hand on Golden's massive shoulder.

"I'll thank you to keep your hands off my prisoner," said Steelman.

"Prisoner?" Sombra's smile was insolent. "Are you certain you brought enough help along to make your arrest, *cabrón?*"

True was afraid her volatile temper was going to get them into worse trouble, so he got her by the arm and pulled her away from Golden and closer to him. Her eyes sparked fire. He shook his head, and she calmed down.

Steelman absorbed the insult with a faint and frosty smile.

"That's the pot calling the kettle black. You folks are outlaws. In fact, this man here is wanted for murder in Louisiana. He was a slave, and killed a white man. They don't like to let that kind of thing go unpunished. Might give other slaves wrong notions."

"That was a long time ago," protested True. "And a long way from here."

"A man's past will always catch up with him." Steelman was staring at Golden now, his killer-gray eyes hooded but dull and deadly. He was still pointing the gun at Golden's face. "This weapon is the new Colt Paterson. What they call a repeating pistol. I could put six bullets in you, mister, before I had to reload. And I have the right to do it. Might say it's my bounden duty. Says so right here." He thumped the Bible with his hand, but did not refer to it as he said, "Numbers, Chapter 35. 'The revenger of blood himself shall slay the murderer: when he meeteth him, he shall slay him.' The avenger of blood." Steelman smiled. "Reckon that's me."

True looked at Chance. "Can't believe you ride with such men."

"They're good men," snapped Chance, bristling. "Brave men. Without them there wouldn't be a Republic of Texas."

With a cold twist in his guts, True saw it clear then.

His brother had become just like Steelman and Hule. Maybe the murder of their family had turned him that way. He would show no mercy, take no prisoners. He lived to kill in the name of the Republic, and he wouldn't be particular about his victims, because the safety of Texas was just an excuse to wreak vengeance. Chance Bowen was a bonafide Ranger now. A man True did not know, or want to know.

"Let's cut a few corners off this small talk," said Hule impatiently. "We know what we're gonna do with the nigger, Cap'n. But what about these two?"

Steelman spoke to Golden. "That's up to you."

"What does that mean?" asked Golden woodenly.

"We've known about you being out in this neck of the woods. Known for quite a spell. There's still a warrant for you across the Sabine. We can kill you here and now, or haul you back and let them exalt you from the nearest tree, compliments of the Republic of Texas."

"I don't believe that," said Golden. "It was thirty years ago I killed that man. You had to go lookin' for that, so's you could hold it over me."

"You're right smart. That's just what we did. Because you're a damned Comanchero, and you know where Helltown is."

Golden nodded. "So that's it."

"That's it. So you can meet your Maker—or cooperate."

"What do you want me to do?"

"Take a couple of my men into Helltown. Vouch for them as outlaw renegades. Rest of us will tag along, a day behind. I don't reckon thirty strangers could just sashay in there without so much as a by-your-leave. But two men ought to be able to get in, take a good look around, and slip back out when the time is right. They'll be able to tell me how many Comancheros there are, and the layout of Helltown. With that information, I'll know better how to mount a successful attack."

Steelman closed the Bible and laid his hand on it like he was taking an oath. "That was the original plan. Seeing as how you have a remuda of horses out there in the corral, we're going to change it, slightly. The two Rangers will take those mustangs into Helltown, like genuine *mesteñeros*. You'll tell the Comancheros they're your new partners."

"How do you know I won't double-cross you?"

"I can think of several reasons. If you cooperate, and survive, you'll win your freedom. The Republic of Texas will inform the State of Louisiana that you're dead and buried, so they can close the books on that murder. You'll be left strictly alone, with a clean slate. If you betray my men, you'll be hounded by every Ranger in Texas. That is, assuming Sergeant Hule and Private Bowen don't manage to kill you first.

"There's one other reason. If my two men are killed, that woman standing behind you will also die. She'll be my hostage. If you don't care what happens to you, maybe you care about her."

"Don't do it, Golden," said True.

"Shut up," growled Hule.

"Chance, Quill Eason knows Hule's a ranger."

"*Shut up!*" raged Hule, hauling off and hitting True square in the face.

With Sombra's help, True got up off the floor, wiping blood from a split lip. Chance hadn't moved. He didn't look at all sorry Hule had hammered his brother.

"He doesn't know what he's talkin' about," Hule assured Steelman. "Sure, I was in Goliad when the Easons killed Rutherford. But Quill Eason never got a look at me. He was running away, like the dirty yellow coward he is, when I got off my one shot at him. All he knows about Jack Hule is that a Ranger by that name spent six months looking for his sorry ass."

"Don't take those horses, Chance," muttered True. "They're meant for a trade with the Comanche Black Wolf, to get Sadie free."

Chance's face twisted at the mention of their sister's name.

"Sadie's dead."

"She ain't! You don't know that."

"Good as."

"What are you saying?"

"He's sayin' your sister is a damned squaw," yelled Hule, his face dark and ugly with anger. "She's laid with stinkin' Yamparika bucks. She ain't fit to be a white woman no more."

True plowed into him. Hule tried to split his skull with the Colt Paterson, but True slipped under and hit low, the only way to bring a big man down. They fell. True hurt him with a punch to the side of the head, and got away before Hule could get hold of him. Hule was almost as big as Golden, six feet and then some of horseshoe iron and old whang leather, and True wasn't going to give him the opportunity to snap his neck like he would a brittle twig.

The action distracted Steelman, and Golden made his move. He rose, overturning the table, and spilling Steelman in the process, shoving the table on top of the Ranger captain. Chance swung his pistol in Golden's direction. Golden hefted the bench he'd been sitting on and hurled it at Chance. The impact slammed Chance across the room. He smashed headlong into the picket wall, and brought most of it down, so much splintered kindling.

"Sombra!" roared Golden. "Bar the door!"

Hule was growling like a gutshot grizzly. Sprawled on the floor, he opted to shoot True and be done with it. He was lining up the Colt when True kicked it out of his grasp.

The tide turned quickly. Sombra almost got the crossbar in place on the door, but the Rangers outside were men drawn without second thought to the sound of a fight, and it was Lon who hit the door first, full force, driving it open and sending Sombra sprawling backward. At the same instant, Steelman shoved the table away and shot Golden.

When he saw Golden fall, the fight went out of True. He dropped to his knees beside the black man, sick to his stomach with the fear that his friend was dead. Rolling Golden over, he was relieved to see otherwise. The bullet had struck Golden in the upper arm. He had a hand clamped over the wound. Blood was streaming through his blunt fingers. A grimace of pain wrenched at his features.

Sombra pushed past Steelman, who had gotten up and was brushing off his preacher's coat. She bent low over Golden, cradling his head in her arms.

"He'll live," said Steelman. "He's worth more to me alive than dead."

True felt the barrel of a gun pressed roughly against the nape of his neck.

"I'm gonna send you direct to hell, True Bowen," snarled Hule.

"Ease off, Sergeant," barked Steelman.

But Hule was wall-eyed mad. He ignored the captain. True heard the Colt's hammer click as it was thumbed back.

"Wait!" breathed Golden through clenched teeth. "Call off your dog, Captain. Let Bowen live, and I'll take you to Helltown."

Steelman pointed his gun at Hule.

"I gave you an order, Sergeant Hule."

Hule took the gun away, and True began to breathe again.

❧ ❧ ❧

They tied True up and propped him in the back corner of the room, sitting on the floor. About the only thing he could move was an eyelash.

Sombra was permitted to tend to Golden's gunshot wound. The bullet had missed the bone and passed right through. Sombra cleaned the wound with hot water, cauterized it with a knife blade heated in the fire, then bound it with her red sash.

Steelman took Hule and Chance outside, leaving Lon to guard True and the others. The Ranger leaned against the wall near the front door, gun in hand, watching every move Sombra and Golden made.

Chance returned later, nodded at Lon and crossed to True, giving Golden a hateful glance in passing. One side of his face was discolored and swollen, the eye half-shut. He hunkered down in front of True and glowered, sullen as a bogged mule.

"True, you're a complete fool."

"Go to hell."

"You shouldn't ought to cuss," he said, mocking True. "What would Ma say?"

"You're going to die, Chance."

"I won't go down alone."

"Spoken like a true Ranger." It wasn't a compliment.

"You used to want to join up with us. That's all you used to talk about."

"I didn't know any better."

"We're leaving at daybreak." Chance glanced over his shoulder at Sombra. "That Mex girl mean anything to you?"

"Yes," snapped True.

"You've gone all the way wrong, True."

"Do tell. . . ." True laughed bitterly.

Chance stood quickly, offended. "When this is over, don't come back east. Far as I'm concerned, you're just another damned Comanchero, and you'll be treated as such."

"One question," said True, stopping Chance in the process of turning away. "Last summer you wouldn't go after the Comanches who had Sadie. Said it was suicide for thirty Rangers to ride out onto the Staked Plains. Now here you are, fixin' to do just that. Thirty Rangers to take on all the Comancheros in Helltown. Not to mention the whole Comanche nation. You wouldn't do it for our sister. Why are you doing it now?"

Chance laid a hand on the Colt Paterson stuck in his belt.

"This new pistol changes everything. We can fight from horseback now. Before, we had to dismount so's we could reload after every shot. Now we can fire without having to reload. That means we can hit 'em hard and fast. We can take on a much larger force and whup 'em."

"It's still suicide."

"With these guns we can win. We're not just thirty men. Cap'n Steelman hand-picked the best fighters in the Republic. We'll ride into the valley of the shadow, True, and strike a blow for Texas."

True understood Chance and his *compadres*, then. They were men who would gladly give their lives for a shot at bloody vengeance.

One thing was certain. If he ever got Sadie back—and the odds looked mighty tall now—he sure couldn't leave her in his brother's care and keeping. Assuming Chance survived Helltown, he wasn't ever going to have anything to do with her. In his mind, Sadie *was* dead. Having a sister who had lived with Comanches would be altogether too humiliating for high and mighty Ranger Chance Bowen.

A little while after Chance left, Sombra picked up Golden's Bible, and came to kneel beside True. Leaning over, she kissed him. A long and lingering kiss. She laid the Bible on the floor close beside him.

"Golden and I will be going with them, True. You're being left behind. But with the map Golden drew, you can find your way to Helltown."

"Why is Steelman leaving me here?"

"He doesn't need you. You'd just be trouble. And maybe he's afraid you might influence your brother. When we go, in the morning, you will be released. The Rangers will take all the horses and guns, so Steelman isn't worried that you might follow."

"How will I?" asked True, discouraged. "At least as Steelman's prisoner I'd get that much closer to Helltown. And we'd be together, Sombra. When the Rangers get there, the killing will start. I…I don't want to lose you."

She looked over her shoulder at Lon. He was watching from across the room, out of earshot if they kept their voices pitched to a whisper. When she looked back at True, fierce determination flamed in her eyes. True braced himself, knowing he wasn't going to like what she was about to say.

"They'll never get to Helltown. Not all of them. Just the two spies who enter as mustangers. I cannot say for certain, but I think I will be the one who enters with them, with Golden staying behind as Steelman's hostage. We can convince Steelman that it would be better to send me. That Golden is such a desperate man he might sacrifice me. Steelman can see Golden means a lot to me. He is confident I won't betray him."

"But you're going to, aren't you?" asked True.

"Yes. The Comancheros will be ready when Steelman attacks. If he does. The Rangers won't have a prayer."

"One of those two Rangers going in will be my brother. That seems to have been decided already. The Comancheros will kill him."

"No, they won't. I will keep him alive."

"You'll keep him alive? How?"

She gazed at him a moment, struggling to find the right words.

"True, I wanted to tell you this before. I never found the courage. I was afraid you would hold the truth against me. After all, the Comanches murdered your family, and they are aided and encouraged by the Helltown Comancheros." She took a long breath. "Rodrigo Shay, the *patrón* of Helltown, the Lord of the Comancheros, is my father."

True stared at her.

My father is a very powerful man, she had once told him. *Ruthless, but fair in his own way.* And he remembered Gancho's remark to her—*I forgot whose blood flows in your veins*—when, in the border-town cantina, she had laid her fancy knife to his throat. The statement had meant nothing to True then. Now it made sense.

She squeezed his arm, frightened. "Say that you don't hate me!"

"I could never hate you, Sombra."

She smiled gratefully.

"But I'm afraid Steelman will kill Golden when he finds out you've warned your father," said True.

She bit down on her lower lip. "There is a risk, but this is the only way. Maybe we can save Golden. Instead of waking one morning to find his two spies have returned, Steelman may find instead that he is surrounded by a hundred Comancheros. Perhaps he will be sensible enough to trade Golden for your brother, and the freedom to leave the Staked Plains alive. I will do everything I can to save Golden."

"Does he know about this?"

"Of course. You heard us whispering as I tended his wound. It is his plan. Oh, True, it tears at my heart to leave you!"

Again she bent over to kiss him. This time she slipped the Spanish knife from under her jacket and tucked it beneath his leg, her movements so circumspect that Lon suspected nothing.

"I promise we will be together again someday," she said. "But we must stop the Rangers from destroying Helltown. Not for my father, but for your sister. This way, we will still have the mustangs to trade for her."

"I have a promise of my own," said True grimly. "I don't know how, but I'll get to Helltown. Just keep looking for me, Sombra. One day you'll see me, coming on."

12

True lay in wait for the stallion, belly-down on the stout limb of a tree, twenty feet above the trail down which the white would bring his *manada* to the creek. Remembering what Sombra had taught him—that mustangs came to the water at the same time every day—he didn't expect to wait long.

The smell of a man or animal in a tree does not drift groundward, but just to be safe, he had crushed sprigs of scrub cedar all over his buckskins. Scent would not give him away. There was, however, a chance that the stallion might see him; the post oak in which he waited had long ago shed every single leaf. So he kept completely still, in spite of being cold and uncomfortable. The afternoon was overcast, the wind wet and cold.

True tried to keep his mind on the task at hand, but he kept thinking about the events of that morning. Standing in front of the rock house, he had watched the Rangers leave, taking Sombra and Golden and the horses with them. Lightning, too. Not to mention his Hawken rifle and Bowie knife.

Sombra's Spanish knife, a long buffalo hide reata Golden had made, another catch-rope, and Golden's pirate eyeglass were all that was left to him. Most importantly, he had Golden's Bible, with the map that would show him the way to Helltown.

The beat of many hooves set his pulse to racing.

The wild horses were coming.

He checked the reata. One end was tied to the limb, the other shaken out into a loop. Golden had promised it was strong enough to stop and hold a full-grown bull buffalo. True prayed that was so. He had the other catch-rope over his shoulder. The plan was to snag the white to the tree with the reata, jump down, and use the other catch-rope to get the stallion by the forefeet.

The white was in the lead as the band came through the trees at a high lope. It took True's breath away, seeing him again. He was bigger, stronger, more striking than the shaggy, sinewy mustangs that followed his lead. True steeled himself for the struggle that lay ahead.

He tried to gauge as best he could the white's speed in relation to the distance and the angle and the time it would take to make the throw. One shot—that was all he would have. Once the stallion realized this watering place was no longer safe, he would take his mares elsewhere and never return.

He made the throw.

The stallion screamed as the loop settled neatly over his head. He reared, twisted, plunged sideways. The mares turned tail. The white tried to follow, jerking savagely against the line that held him, so hard in fact that he fell to the ground, his legs going out from under him.

True let out a jubilant whoop that could have been heard at the rock house two miles down-creek.

The stallion rose and lunged with all his might against the line. The limb broke with a crack louder than a rifle shot, and True was falling.

Impact with the ground knocked all the air out of his lungs. Stunned, he rolled over and tried to get up. The broken limb, bigger around than one of Golden's arms, came flying to hit him in the head, knocking him into the dirt again.

He almost blacked out. A loud buzzing filled his head. He could feel blood pouring out of his nose, its copper taste filling his mouth. The ground seemed to be spinning madly beneath him. Then it began to vibrate. He looked up to see the stallion heading straight for him.

He will turn on you like a trapped panther. He will do his best to kill you.

True powered to his feet and made a diving lunge for the nearest tree trunk.

The stallion was quicker. Horse and man collided. Again True fell. The stallion spun, eyes blazing, ears back, mouth open. His head dipped as he struck like a rattler. Big blunt teeth caught True's left leg below the knee. They ripped through the leggins and gouged a patch of skin and then snapped together, sounding like a sprung wolf trap as True rolled desperately away.

The stallion reared, walking on his hind legs, front hooves slashing the air. The broken limb, still attached to the reata, came bouncing over the ground as the white rose up, and struck True between the shoulder blades. True got hold of it and threw it at the stallion, hitting the white between the eyes. With a fierce scream the stallion lit out at that faster-than-a-gallop pace of his.

Without thinking, True latched onto the broken limb as it careened past.

The stallion dragged him up the trail as though he weighed no more than a sack of feathers. True went skittering over the ground, ricocheting off tree trunks, bounced up and slammed down. It was a rough ride.

When the stallion suddenly veered off the trail, slipping between a pair of hackberries, True saw his chance. He managed to bring the broken limb down parallel with the ground, so that it struck against the two tree trunks like a gate pole against two posts.

This time the limb didn't break. The stallion hit the end of the line and fell. For a few precious seconds the reata went slack. True whipped the Spanish knife from his belt, cut the reata from the limb and tied off to the bigger of the two hackberries.

The stallion rose and gave a tremendous shake, testing the line with a few sharp head jerks that made the length of buffalo hide hum like a plucked guitar string.

Then he just stood there, pawing the ground and snorting.

True stumbled out of the stallion's reach, trying to catch his breath, testing his bruised, scraped body, and wondering what in tarnation he was going to do with the white, now that he had him.

In the fall from the tree, or the dragging that followed, True had lost the other catch-rope. He went back to find it. Returning to the stallion, he stepped out bold as new brass, swinging a loop. The stallion started crow-hopping. True tossed the loop in the throw mustangers called the *mangana*, and nabbed the horse by the fore-feet. The stallion fell, thrashed, and finally lay still, sides heaving. True dallied the catch-rope around another tree, at right angles to the buffalo hide reata.

While he sat a safe distance from the white, some of the mares began to slip cautiously closer through the trees. The stallion heard them, and struggled to stand. He let out a long, drawn-out whinny, and the mares hightailed it out of there. True sensed that he was telling them to save themselves.

Returning to the rock house, True gathered up a buffalo robe, the Bible, a wooden bucket, a pouch of venison jerky, and Golden's pirate eyeglass. He camped that night within sight of the stallion.

Sleep eluded him. He kept thinking about Sombra and Golden. They were both risking their lives on his account. Somehow he had to get to Helltown before the killing started. Somehow he had to save them both, and rescue Sadie.

He spent hours studying Golden's map by the light of his fire, committing it to memory.

The next morning, the stallion was standing, magnificent head held high and proud, eyes flaming with wild ferocity. When True moved closer, doing his best to "horse talk" like he had seen Golden do, the stallion acted up, snorting and back-kicking and tripping over the ropes. Afraid that the horse would break a leg, True backed off. He went down to the creek and fetched water in the bucket. This he set down within the stallion's reach.

All that day True sat and watched the white. The stallion cropped not a blade of grass, drank not a drop of water.

After several days of this, True realized what the stallion was up to. The horse would not eat or drink as long as he was held captive. He preferred death to submission.

A cold drizzle fell throughout the fourth day. Soaked to the skin, True huddled in the buffalo robe and longed for the warmth and shelter the rock house would provide.

The following day the wind turned southerly. The sky was a brilliant blue, the air warm and pleasant. The bare limbs of the creek-bottom trees clacked and clattered in a gentle breeze carrying the first scent of spring.

Spring had always before been a time of new hope and high spirits for True. Not so, this go-round. He kept thinking about the Comancheros. He could visualize the long trains of *carretas*, laden with guns and whiskey and tobacco, striking out across the high plains from Santa Fe, bound for Helltown. He could see the mustangers driving their herds to the same destination. He could imagine the Comanches striking the lodges of their winter camps, loading their goods onto travois and bending their steps toward the rendezvous site.

Each time True approached the stallion, the white would go into a frenzy. He did not know how to bend the horse to his will. But the stallion was his only hope. To set out on foot would be futile, considering the distance involved. No other single mustang would do in trade for Sadie.

True gradually stopped eating and drinking himself. For long periods of time he would drift away in a kind of numb, semiconscious state.

The morning of the seventh day—or was it the eighth? True had lost track of time—the stallion's soft and persistent whickering shook him out of delirium. Now and again the white would throw back his head and cut loose with a shrill whinny. This went on for hours.

The stallion was neighing his death song.

True struggled weakly to his feet. Shrugging off the buffalo robe, he staggered toward the suffering horse, Sombra's Spanish knife in hand. He was shaking like a leaf, and cold sweat drenched his clothes. Burning up with fever, he could scarcely see straight.

The stallion stood quite still, watching True's every move. The horse was ganted now, his ribs sticking out. But he had lost none of his stubborn pride. He stood tall and unbowed, willing to die for freedom.

This time, as True drew close, the white didn't kick up a fuss.

With a heavy heart, True laid the knife against the stallion's throat.

And cut the buffalo-hide reata.

Then he dropped to his knees and slashed the tight loop binding the animal's forefeet.

The stallion didn't move.

"Go on," said True. "You win. You're free. Go on."

He got to his feet, somehow, reeled back to the buffalo robe, and collapsed.

When he next opened his eyes, True didn't know if it was that same day, the day after, or a week later.

He saw dark shapes in the trees above him. He squinted, blinked, and tried to focus on those shapes.

Turkey vultures.

He was laughing at them when he heard the howl of a wolf. Sitting up quickly, he spotted one slinking away through the underbrush. A rustling sound snapped his head around. Another lobo emerged from cover, not thirty feet away, head lowered, mouth peeled back in a snarl. A low-pitched, rumbling growl welled up in its throat.

Grasping the knife, True managed to stand, and braced himself against a tree. The wolf stepped closer. From an eye-corner, True saw a streak of gray fur in distant brush, off to one side. More wolves, circling him. He kept his attention on the lobo in front.

"Come on," he croaked. "How'd you like a bellyful of Toledo steel?"

The wolf lunged with a drawn-out surly growl, and was halfway home when the white stallion came from nowhere, full-tilt, uttering a shrill scream.

The wolf veered sharply away. The stallion was too quick, and ran the lobo over. The wolf went sprawling. The stallion twisted in midair and came down with front hooves slashing. The trampled wolf was hurt, and slow getting up. The hooves struck him squarely in the head. He fell, dying, in a scarlet spray of blood.

Overhead, the disturbed buzzards flapped away.

Another lobo came at True from the side, a streak of silver-gray fur and yellow fangs.

The wolf leaped for his throat. True cast an arm up and caught the lobo below the muzzle. Jaws snapped shut inches from his face, saliva stinging his eyes. Driven to the ground by the wolf's weight, he drove the knife to the hilt into the animal's belly, and ripped it open.

The rest of the pack gave up the fight. True wasn't sure how many of them there were in all—he saw only a couple as they retreated. The stallion chased one, but was back by the time True had gotten to his feet.

True stood there for a full minute staring at the stallion in disbelief.

Holding his breath, he took a tentative step forward. The stallion whickered, and backed up.

It dawned on True then. He was covered with lobo's blood.

"It's the blood smell, ain't it, boy? Well, you wait right there. I can take care of that." Heart pounding, he headed for the creek; turned once to throw back, "Don't go away, now."

He washed off in the brisk water of the brawling run.

The stallion was waiting right where he had been before.

True eased closer, expecting the horse to bolt. At arm's length, he reached out to touch the stallion's neck. Moving ever so slowly, he ran his hand over the mustang's shoulder, across the ribs, flank and haunch. The stallion didn't move except to turn his head and watch.

When True tried to put the buffalo robe on the horse's back, hoping to use it as a kind of saddle, the stallion snorted and sidestepped. So True left the robe behind. Knife and eyeglass under his belt, the reata over his shoulder, and the Bible under his shirt, he grabbed a handful of mane and swung aboard. Instead of catapulting True into the trees, the horse stood stock-still.

The white's long, flowing mane hung down both sides of his neck. True took a handful from either side, wondering if he would use the hair like reins to turn the stallion.

At the slightest touch of True's heels, the stallion set out, pacing through the trees, splashing across the creek, responding without complaint as True steered with a tug on one side of the mane or the other.

As horse and rider left the creek-bottom trees, the turkey vultures returned to their perch, near where the dead wolves lay.

New hope surging through him, True set a course north-by-northwest, making for the Staked Plains.

Somewhere in that sea of grass stood Helltown.

13

Near the windswept rim of the Cap Rock, True sat the white stallion and gazed for some time at Helltown, off in the distance.

The Comanchero stronghold was perched on an arrowhead mesa formed by the convergence of two steep-sided canyons. No horse could negotiate the red cliffs protecting Helltown on three sides. It would be a tough and chancy climb for a strong and agile man. The only good access was a trail coming off the high plains and across the mesa from the west.

According to Golden, Helltown had long ago been a Spanish mission, built shortly after the first *conquistadores* ventured north from Old Mexico. This was prior to the Comanche migration south, when the Apaches and Padoucas laid claim to the Staked Plains. Jesuit priests had thought to civilize the Apaches and Padoucas, and learned the hard way that Comanches were not as easy to civilize as the tribes that had gone before them. After a dozen Spaniards were tortured and murdered by the warlike Komantcia, the mission was abandoned.

Decades later, Rodrigo Shay decided the derelict mission would serve Comanchero purposes quite well. In short order, Helltown became the foremost rendezvous between Comanche and Comanchero.

True used the pirate eyeglass for a closer look. A high tan adobe wall completely encircled the mission-turned-fortress, blocking from view any activity within. Something was going on in there, though, for pale yellow dust lifted into the blue vault of sky. The old

94

chapel's belfry, higher than the perimeter wall, rose from the center of the compound. From there, a lookout could see a half-day's ride in any direction.

True wondered if there was a sentry up there now, and if he had already been discovered, and what the Comanchero reaction to his presence would be.

Only one way to find out.

Snugging the eyeglass back under his belt, he tapped his heels against the stallion's side, and the horse swung directly into its smooth pace.

True had traveled seven days from the rock house, on the move virtually around the clock. The tireless stallion had never slacked off the pace. With precious little graze or water, after a week of captivity during which he had grazed and watered not at all, the horse carried True mile after mile and day after day, out of the brasada, through rugged limestone hills, across dry mesquite prairie, and finally over the Cap Rock escarpment and onto the high grasslands of the Staked Plains.

Golden's map etched in his mind, True kept pretty much to the rim of the Cap Rock, the eastern edge of the Llano Estacado. He hoped, by moving day and night, to reach Helltown not too far behind Steelman and the others.

The endless plains stretched away to the north and west. An immense sea of grass, with scarcely a tree to break the monotony. There were chaparral and mesquite bush, occasional clumps of yucca and catclaw. Grama and buffalo grass was new and green and plentiful.

The plains were vast but far from empty. An abundance of quail and larks existed on them, and True saw plenty of cottontails, huge colonies of prairie dogs, and more rattlers than he cared to. Roving packs of wolves and herds of antelope kept their distance. Sometimes he would spot far-off bands of wild horses, but the stallion showed no inclination to leave him and take up again the wild free life of a mustang. Every night, coyotes by the dozen made song.

There were buffalo, too. Vast herds of them, sometimes stretching as far as the eye could see. Having split into small bunches for the winter, the shaggies were beginning to congregate. They moved slowly through a haze of lazy dust, grazing peacefully. Massive beasts, with tremendous humps and shoulders covered with thick black-brown hair. Their eyes were small and reddish. The bulls had short white horns, sharply curved. The air would be heavy with the warm and musky smell of them.

Water was scarce on the high plains, where rivers were rare as hen's teeth. Fortunately for True, warm spring showers danced lightly across the grassland twice that week, depositing a few inches of murky liquid, instantly alive with wigglers, in the bottoms of buffalo wallows.

He saw nary a soul during the entire journey. This was a big and lonesome country. Not that he minded. The only souls he was likely to see out here were Comanche or Comanchero. True was duly grateful for Golden's map. He would never have found his way across this uncharted land without it.

He ate what was left of the venison jerky. He slept on the back of the stallion. Sometimes he would get down and walk, stretching his legs, and leading the horse by the mane.

Reaching the rim of the canyon south of Helltown, True turned west, and eventually discovered a precarious game trail sidewinding down into a branch canyon. The stallion proved to be as surefooted as a mountain goat. Crossing the gorge, he came upon several strong springs nourishing rock pools, and a well-established trace twisting up a draw to the top of the mesa and the road into Helltown.

The Comancheros relied on these canyon springs for water, using mule trains and casks for transport. Ascending the trace, winding up shale slopes spotted with scrub cedar, True saw shards of wood among the bones of an unfortunate jack which had slipped and fallen a hundred feet down the steep slope.

Reaching the top of the mesa, he found the red dust of the rim-rock road marked by the recent passage of many unshod ponies, and creased by the foot-wide wheels of heavily laden *carretas*.

He turned east and rode on toward Helltown.

Drawing near his destination, he heard a bell clanging, and saw men moving on the high west wall. The main gate, age-blackened beams of wood cross-hatched with strap-iron and set into a wide adobe arch, opened slightly to spew forth a half-dozen hardcases. True rode on into their midst before stopping the stallion.

The Comancheros fanned out across the road. All carried at least one pistol and one knife. A few cradled rifles in their arms. One carried an old blunderbuss, its flaring muzzle as big as the gaping mouth of a ten-pound bass.

A short, burly character ventured too close, and the stallion snapped at him, ripping the sleeve of his shoddy shirt. The man danced away, dark stubbled features turning several shades darker as his compadres laughed.

"Hey, gringo," he said, glowering at True as he rubbed his arm where the stallion's blunt teeth had grazed the skin. "Are you lost?"

"Come to see Rodrigo Shay," replied True, struggling with his Spanish.

The man frowned. Pushing the floppy brim of his sombrero out of small, furtive eyes, he glanced down the road, and looked puzzled. He couldn't believe a lone Texican would have the gall to ride so brazenly into Helltown.

"Perhaps Rodrigo Shay does not want to see you," he said, hitching up a broad leather belt that hosted a flintlock pistol and double-edged belduque.

"I reckon he will. It's my intention to one day marry his daughter."

The Comancheros found this statement highly amusing.

The spokesman abruptly stopped laughing, and made a sharp arm motion.

"Get down off that horse, gringo, and we will talk some more." The clatter of hammers rolled back was loud in True's ears.

One of the men was trying to get around behind. The stallion turned his head away from the spokesman to watch this offside threat. The spokesman saw his chance and lunged. Strong hands latched onto True and dragged him off the horse. True hit him in the face with an elbow as he went down. The Comanchero lurched backward. The stallion, snorting, reared as the other men closed in, giving them pause with flailing hooves.

True hit the ground, bounced back up with Sombra's knife in hand. The spokesman, swaying, was trying to yank the pistol from his belt. True lowered his head and rammed into him. Both men went down. They kicked up a cloud of dust, scuffling, until True managed to open the Comanchero's thigh up with the knife. Squealing like a stuck pig, the man thrashed, scarlet spurts of blood leaving dark smears in the dirt. True broke away from him and whirled, flinching, as a gun went off.

Quill Eason stood in the road, a thread of white smoke rising from the barrel of a horse pistol pointed skyward.

"The shivaree is over," he drawled. "Boys, if you had kilt this feller, Rodrigo Shay would've had your *huevos* cut off and fed to the hogs." He nodded pleasantly at True. "Howdy, Bowen. Been a long time."

"Howdy, Quill. Seems you're always saving my bacon."

"It was these boys I was trying to save. The ones you hadn't killed, Shay sure would have."

Just then Sombra slipped out of Helltown's gate. Rushing past Quill, raven hair streaming out behind, she launched herself at True, almost knocking him off his feet. Holding her again felt mighty fine to True, but all this affection, displayed before an audience of strangers, had him blushing.

"Sombra!" he gasped, between kisses. "Now simmer down ... !"

"I knew you would come."

"Wish you'd told these fellers."

Anger swirling in her eyes, she stepped away from him to stand with hands on hips, watching the wounded Comanchero squirming in the dust.

"Idiot!" she said. "Did my father not instruct you to watch for this man?"

"Help me!" he groaned. "I am bleeding to death."

"We wished only to check him for weapons," explained another submissively. "As we are told to do with all strangers. But he would not dismount."

"He didn't want to get shot, accidental-like," commented Quill dryly. "Whoever killed him got the horse, right?"

Sombra addressed the other Comancheros. "Take this worthless *cabrón* inside, and see that he does not die. My father may wish to skin him alive, later."

She turned a bright smile on True as a couple of Comancheros carted the wounded man through the gate. Then her gaze slipped to the stallion behind True, and saucered with astonishment as she recognized the horse.

"*El Blanco!*" she gasped.

She moved like a sleepwalker past True. The stallion snorted and started to hoolihan. True hurried over, and calmed the white. Sombra watched in utter disbelief.

"True," she breathed. "How…?"

"You didn't expect me to walk all that way, did you?"

Quill laughed softly. "I like your style, True Bowen."

"Tell me what's happened?" True asked her, anxious for an answer to the question that had tormented him for more than a fortnight. "My brother. Is he…?"

"Alive. Come. I will take you to him."

"Golden. What about Golden?"

She looked away, squeezing her eyes into slits against the blinding brightness of the sun, and against the pain in her heart.

"The Rangers still have him. But I believe he is still alive. I refuse to believe otherwise. We arrived only two days ago. Steelman will still be waiting for his spies to return. There is yet time to save Golden."

True followed her and Quill through the gate. He had a handful of the stallion's mane, but wasn't really leading the horse; the white was content to walk along beside him.

The plaza of the Comanchero stronghold covered three acres, rectangular in shape. On the north and east sides were rows of adobe huts, built cheek by jowl and flush against the perimeter wall. They resembled barracks, and their flat roofs served as ramparts.

The chapel stood on the south side. The structure had suffered from long years of neglect after its abandonment by the Spaniards and subsequent acquisition by the Comancheros. Much of the roof had caved in, but the belfry True had seen from a distance looked sturdy enough. Beside the chapel were several large corrals.

Helltown was bustling with activity. Men, women, and children filled the plaza. Mustangs milled in a corral. More than twenty *carretas* were scattered around. True guessed that a train had arrived earlier in the day, for some of the Comanchero freighters were unloading their goods, while others were unyoking teams of oxen. The beasts were driven into another corral.

The *carreta* was customarily drawn by five or six yoke. Its most arresting feature was the single set of massive wooden wheels. Fashioned from three huge sections of wood, the wheels stood taller than the average man. The three sections were held together with long wooden pins, stout as a man's arm, passed through bored holes rim to rim. The fifteen-foot bed was lashed with rawhide to a single heavy axle. Some *carretas* had solid sideboards, and a few sported thatch or canvas roofing. When the ox teams were removed, the *carreta* was tilted forward to rest on the tongue.

Crossing the full length of the plaza, True and the stallion were objects of intense curiosity. Small groups of rough-hewn mustangers pointed and put their heads together. They knew well the legend of the White Pacer.

Peering at the Comanchero families, True's first impression was that they were a pretty poor-looking lot. Many of the children were naked, or nearly so. Barefoot, tangle-haired women crouched in front of *brasseros*—adobe ovens—baking johnnycake, boiling beans, roasting prairie dog and jackrabbit on spits, and shooing away gaunt mongrel dogs. One woman stood in the doorway of a hut, nursing her infant child. Two boys were having at each other in a dust-raising slugfest. Adults stood about like spectators at a cockfight. Over in a corner of the plaza, several men were engaged in a shooting match, driving nails into a post with long guns at thirty paces. Horsemen, hard glinting eyes in their sun-blackened faces, rode closer to have a look-see at True and the stallion, only to quirt their nimble mounts away at the merest glance from Sombra, the daughter of Helltown's lord and master.

Thinking twice, True wondered if he was in any condition to judge these people by their appearance. He didn't exactly cut a fine figure himself. He was every bit as dark and dusty as they. His auburn hair brushed the ragged blanket-serape covering his shoulders. The soles of his boots had more holes in them than a dead hero. His buckskin leggins were tattered rags hanging off his bony legs.

It occurred to him that he fit in right nicely with these renegades. He wondered if Sadie would even recognize him.

They stopped at a hut at the end of the south wall row. One small window was set with thick straps of iron. The door was heavy wood, barred on the outside.

"Your brother is in there," said Sombra.

"I want to go in."

"It would be better if you spoke to him through the window. I am afraid he will try something foolish if we open the door. And then he would die."

True moved closer to the window. Gripping the strap-iron, he looked in. The hut was dark and dank. A sour smell filled his nostrils. At first he couldn't see a thing.

"Chance? Chance, it's me, True."

He heard the jangle of iron, a scrape and a rustle.

Chance appeared, and stared at True like he was seeing a ghost. His lip was cut and swollen. A purple-rimmed gash, caked with blood, decorated his left eye. When he reached up to clutch the strap-iron with both hands, True saw the heavy shackles, red with rust, clamped to his wrists.

"Well," said True, forcing a smile. "I see they didn't take you without a fight."

"True," he muttered hoarsely, "you shouldn't be here, dammit."

"Don't worry about me."

Chance looked past him, at Sombra. His face twisted, and his mouth curved into a sneer.

"Goddamn bitch…"

"Thanks to her you're still alive," snapped True.

"I'd rather they'd killed me, like they done for Lon."

"Lon? I thought Hule—"

"Cap'n Steelman changed his mind about sending Hule. Had to do with Hule's blood feud against Eason there. The cap'n was afraid Hule might muddy the water and give himself away, he's so primed to put that sonuvabitch under the ground."

True glanced at Quill, who touched the brim of his hat, standing hipshot off to one side, and wearing that buccaneer smile of his.

"Least Lon went down fighting, like a Ranger should," grumbled Chance. "Too bad I can't say likewise."

"You and your damned Rangers," said True, disgusted.

Chance was shocked, then resentful.

"I guess it's plain whose side you're on. I'm glad our folks are dead, so's they don't have to know this. That their son is a goddamn Comanchero."

"I am not Comanchero," replied True, angrily spacing each word. "I am here for one reason. To get our sister back. And if you say she's dead, or good as, one more time, I'm going to come in there and whup you to a slim frazzle."

"You truck with Comanches, that makes you a Comanchero in my book." He pointed with his chin. "Look yonder."

True looked. Across the dust-hazed plaza, men were unloading a *carreta* laden with long, casketlike crates.

"Know what's in them crates?" asked Chance. "Rifles. Plenty of powder and shot to go with 'em, too, I'll warrant. All for the Comanches. How many Texans will be killed with those rifles, True?"

"After I get Sadie back, then I'll worry about that."

"A wise decision."

True turned to face a man wearing a white planter's hat, a long fringed buckskin coat and yellow nankeen trousers. A scarlet sash encircled his waist. Instead of boots, he wore beaded moccasins. He was a big man, with brawny shoulders, slab belly, powerful legs. A roan beard and thick eyebrows were dusted with gray. His skin resembled brown parchment. Square-jawed and bull-necked, getting on in years, he didn't have an ounce of softness to him. Still vigorous and keen of mind, the shamrock-green eyes were bright and piercing.

He was smiling faintly at True. "It is always best to see one task through before setting yourself another."

"Doesn't mean I like what's going on here," said True.

"I wouldn't expect you to."

"Father," said Sombra, "this is…"

He held up a hand big as a bear paw to cut her short.

"Yes, I know. True Bowen. In a very brief time, young man, I have heard a great deal about you. I am, as you have probably already surmised, Rodrigo Shay."

14

"You're a dead man, Shay," growled Chance.

Shay stepped closer to the window and peered with cold detachment at True's brother.

"You make a poor spy, Ranger. You nurture your hate, wear your feelings on your sleeve. Had my daughter not betrayed you, you would have betrayed yourself."

Rodrigo Shay wasn't at all the kind of man True had expected him to be. He was well educated, not a rough-edged cutthroat. But True warned himself that beneath this smooth veneer of good breeding and refinement must lurk a ruthless character capable of anything. Only such a man could command the loyalty of the Comancheros.

Shay turned an admiring gaze on the white stallion.

"Tell me, True Bowen, how did you manage to capture a legend?"

"Sombra taught me."

"She taught you many things, did she not?"

True felt his cheeks get hot. "We're going to get married."

"Are you now? Doesn't it bother you that her father is a man hated and feared by your own kind?"

"I don't hold that against her."

Shay laughed, a soft and rasping sound. The sound of a spade striking deep into sandy soil.

"We will talk later. You will dine with us. I should know more about my future son-in-law. For the time being, Eason will keep you company. Sombra, come with me, please."

She wanted to stay, but she didn't argue, and accompanied Shay across the plaza in the direction of the chapel.

"True." It was Chance, at the window. "True, you've got to warn Steelman that Shay knows about him. If they ride in now, they'll be massacred."

"At least they'll die like Rangers," replied True coldly. "Ain't that all that matters?"

"Go to hell."

Quill started walking away. "Come on, True."

The stallion in tow, True followed Eason across the busy plaza. Quill found a spot to his liking near the corrals, behind an unloaded *carreta*, where they could not be overheard. He took a hard look around before speaking.

"You ought to know that Gancho is here. The stunt you pulled down on the border stuck in his craw."

"What stunt?"

"You've got a short memory. You waltzed in, held him and his men at gunpoint, beat him at arm-wrasslin', and took Sombra away. He always liked to think she was his woman. Now, I ain't sayin' they ever sealed the bargain, so to speak," he added quickly, seeing something ominous in True's expression. "Maybe they did, maybe they didn't. But truth is, he was real taken with her. So, naturally, he doesn't hold you in real high regard."

"She came with me of her own free will."

"Never in a hundred years will you convince Gancho that women have any such thing. He's blaming you, and you may as well accept it."

"Okay. I accept it."

What was one more thing to worry about?

"That's why we're here, so early on, without a mockey between us. Gancho's up to no good. See, he figured you would show up here, to try and get your sister away from Black Wolf. He's aimin' to make plenty trouble for you."

"How?"

"Took me a while, but I finally got it out of him. He aims to trade with Black Wolf himself, for your sister. Take her for his own. I don't know exactly how—he hasn't got much to trade with, far as I can see—but he's a savvy cuss. He'll take your sister because you took Sombra away from him. That's the way he thinks."

"Never happen. I'll kill him first."

Quill nodded soberly.

"You may have to do just that, hoss."

"My father was a mariner," said Rodrigo Shay. "He left County Cork at the tender age of nine years to embark on a lifetime committed to adventure. He began as a cabin boy on a trader bound for the Orient. He sailed the seven seas, and rounded the Horn a dozen times. A self-educated man, my father. I inherited his love of literature."

His gesture diverted True's attention to the books that filled a cabinet standing against one wall.

They sat at a long, burnished mahogany table, in what had once been the chapel sacristy—a fairly small room off the main chamber. The sacristy's roof was intact. Huge square beams crossed high overhead. True wondered where the men who built the mission had found such lumber, in a land where a man made his own shade.

Slender white candles burned in silver candelabra. High above, in the rafters gloom, sparrows flittered and chirruped. Occasionally one would land on the table and boldly steal a crumb.

True couldn't hold this larceny against them. He couldn't remember having ever sat down to better bait. Smoked ham, sweet potatoes, fresh baked bread with marmalade. Shay saved the best for himself, it seemed. True heaped a couple of helpings onto a china plate, and relearned how to use a knife and fork. He passed on the pickled herring and brandy Shay said came from France. He drank instead water from the canyon springs, and filled a crystal goblet several times from a scrolled pewter pitcher.

"He later jumped ship in California," continued Shay. "Married the daughter of a Spanish grandee. I am the result." He smiled at

Sombra. "Perhaps that is why my daughter is so strong-willed and short-tempered. Irish and Latin blood make for an explosive mix. True Bowen—you must come from good Irish stock as well. I predict the children you two produce will be holy terrors."

"Father!"

For the first time, True saw Sombra blush.

Sitting across the table from him, she was a double-rectified vision of beauty, clad in a high-necked taffeta dress frilled with lace. True was so accustomed to seeing her in men's clothes, this was quite a shock. Not that he objected to the change. Her braided black hair gleamed richly in the glow from the sweet-scented candles.

"Yes, my daughter is as strong-willed as she is beautiful," said Shay. "She will have her way. And she is jealous of her freedom. As well as the freedom of others. That is why she left me, years ago. She doesn't care for the business I am in. The buying and selling of Comanche captives."

He poured himself more brandy. "She may have told you that she joined a family of *mesteñeros*. I understand they met a harsh fate at the hand of Comanches. Then she took up with Gancho. She would bring the mustangs she captured here to Helltown, and trade them for captives. She would then make arrangements to return those she set free to their home and loved ones."

"If they had a home or loved ones left, after the Comanches were finished," said Sombra crisply.

"This is a war we're fighting, my dear. The Comanches, for all their faults, are our most valuable allies."

"Who are you fighting in this war?" asked True.

"You and yours, True. The war is as yet undeclared. But, inevitably, our respective governments will someday make it official. Your people will not be satisfied until they possess every *vara* of ground between here and the Pacific coast. And Mexico does not intend to give the land up without a struggle. Right now, the Comanches act as a buffer between us."

Shay deftly changed the subject. "But, be that as it may, and whatever our past differences, I am pleased that Sombra has returned to make peace with her father. I was happy to grant her wish that your brother's life be spared. Alas, I could not do his comrade the same favor. My men are like wild dogs—I must throw them a bone every now and then. And I am greatly relieved that Sombra has broken away from Gancho. That man has a cruel streak, and is no respecter of women."

"You could grant me another wish," said Sombra. "You could speak to Black Wolf when he comes, and persuade him to give up True's sister."

"Regretfully, I cannot. I must remain impartial. As the judge and jury of all disputes here, I cannot take sides. I made the rules, I must abide by them. Having said that, I am confident Black Wolf will trade the girl ... for the white stallion."

True glanced at the doorway leading to the main part of the chapel. Open to the sky, it resembled a courtyard. Night had fallen, and two Comancheros sat on their heels around a blazing fire, built in a hole chipped out of the stone floor. They were there to guard the goods.

Crates of rifles and whiskeys were stacked among the rubble of the long-ago roof collapse. There were dozens of casks in which spring water was stored. Enough, Shay had claimed, to supply the Comancheros for a month, were an enemy to besiege Helltown.

Included in the trade goods were knives of tempered Sheffield steel, good woolen blankets from Scotland, imported French fabrics, even tobacco from Southern growers. Most of these goods were transported in sailing ships to California, then moved overland by mule train or *carreta* to Santa Fe, where they were warehoused until the spring leg of the journey to Helltown. It occurred to True that a great many people were profiting from this trade with the Comanches—at the expense of Texas.

But he was thinking less of commerce than he was the white stallion, who stood patiently just beyond the doorway. The horse had followed him right into the chapel, and the only reason he didn't have a place at the table was because he couldn't quite fit through the narrow doorway into the sacristy.

"He follows you like a faithful dog," observed Shay.

"I'm not his master. It's not like that at all. I don't rightly know why he came with me."

"I believe you have become as attached to the stallion as he has become to you."

"Whatever it takes to get Sadie back, I'll do it."

"It is possible that Black Wolf won't come to Helltown this year."

"He'll come. He has to."

"It's also conceivable that he won't want to give your sister up, no matter what the price."

"Then I'll have to try and take her."

"If you try," said Shay, "I will have to stop you. Regardless of my daughter's love for you. If I allowed it, the Comanches would be outraged, and would break all ties with Helltown."

He threw a worried glance at Sombra, asking a silent question. Her face was a blank mask. Only she knew where she would stand if such a conflict arose.

"What about Golden?" asked True curtly.

Shay sat back in his chair, a heavy piece of carved mahogany with red velvet upholstery.

"We ride to meet the Rangers at daybreak."

"You know where they are?"

"Of course. A day's ride. Would you care to come along?"

"You aim to trade my brother for Golden?"

"My daughter wishes me to attempt it. I am willing. I remember Golden. I always liked him. I will take fifty men, in the hope I might discourage the Rangers from making a fight."

"Doesn't sound like you think that'll work."

His eyes were glittering chunks of green ice.

"Rangers have never been, in my experience, men who listened to reason. They *will* fight, I suspect, even against long odds." He smiled ruefully. "They are hard men. Brave men. I cannot help but admire them. But they won't have a prayer."

True thought, He doesn't know about the new revolving pistols.

Which led him to assume that Chance and Lon hadn't carried theirs into Helltown. Made sense, come to think of it. Steelman was smart enough not to show his hand before the bets were laid.

"I'll go with you," he said. "Maybe I can convince them to turn around and haul off for home."

Shay was skeptical. "That would be a remarkable feat." His gaze drifted to the doorway, and he could see the stallion beyond. "But you have done some rather remarkable things already, haven't you? Faced Gancho down. Bearding the lion in his den, so to speak. And you ride a horse that, legend has it, cannot be tamed." He spread his hands. "Maybe you can work another miracle."

He leaned forward suddenly, pointing a blunt finger.

"But heed my words, True Bowen. With Rangers, there is no neutral ground. Either you are for them or against them. And if they decide you are against them, my friend, they will kill you quick as they would a Comanchero."

15

The way it looked to True, with only a few days having passed since Chance and Lon rode into Helltown pretending to be Anglo outlaws-turned-mustangers, Steelman wouldn't have started fretting about them yet. He would realize they might not be able to simply waltz in, take a good look around, and then dust out. Not without raising Comanchero suspicion.

Rodrigo Shay did indeed know exactly where the Rangers were holed up. It took the better part of a day to get there. He, True, and Sombra were accompanied by fifty of the roughest-looking bravos on the frontier.

Quill was not among them. Neither was Gancho. True hadn't seen Gancho since arriving at Helltown, though he kept an eye peeled.

Chance rode right alongside True, his hands lashed to the saddlehorn and his reins in the keeping of a Comanchero in front of them.

Once through the Helltown gate, they rode down the trail past the sweetwater springs, through the canyon still deep in cool morning shadow, and onto the prairie, leaving the heights of the Cap Rock behind. The wind forever rustled through the sagebrush and switch grass. The sky was striped with broad strokes of mare's tail.

At one point True maneuvered the white stallion alongside Sombra's apron-faced sorrel and tried to return the Spanish knife.

"You keep it," she said. "You may need it before this day is done."

"Should anything happen to me, can I count on you to get Sadie away from the Comanch'?"

"You know you can."

Shay did not keep his Comancheros in tight formation. Instead, they flared out for a half-mile on either flank, with a half-dozen ranging far ahead. They held their mounts to a walk throughout the day, which turned quite warm, and paused only twice, and then briefly, to let the horses breathe with loosened girths and then drink from hat crowns filled with water poured from burlap-wrapped gourds.

The sun was nearing the western rim when Shay stopped and motioned his men in. Then he and True walked through tall grass to the rim of the long rise. They did not bother hiding, which was just as well, since the stallion, as usual, followed right along behind True.

"They are there," said Shay, pointing. "In that arroyo hidden in the trees."

True saw the wash snaking through the prairie folds about a quarter-mile east, its course marked by a scatter of black willow bright with new green buds and cottonwoods with their gray limbs still bare. But he saw no sign of thirty-odd Rangers.

"Water down there?" asked True.

"Yes."

"I don't see any birds. This time of year the branches ought to be heavy with them."

Smiling, Shay nodded. "Exactly. Do you still want to do this thing?"

"Yep."

"We will stay out of sight, behind this *loma*. Should you need us to show ourselves, raise your left hand over your head. Should you need us to take action, wave the hand."

"They are my own kind," said True sternly. "I don't reckon I will signal an attack on fellow Texicans."

"Ride in slowly. They know we are here. There is a lookout on the rise beyond the arroyo. Men of action do not care to hide in the brush and wait. They will be nervous, quick on the trigger. Go now; if we are to fight, we would do well to have the sun at our backs."

True went back to fetch his tight-lipped brother. A Comanchero offered a flintlock pistol, as True had no firearm, but he declined. He had no intention of shooting a Ranger. He did, however, accept a parting kiss from Sombra. Then, taking Chance's reins, he rode over the rise and down into the Ranger hideout.

Chance said not a word as they rode into the smattering of trees along the arroyo.

When he did speak, it was to Ranger Hule, who materialized in their path, slipping out of the scrub willow just before they reached the cutbank of the wash.

"Don't shoot," said Chance. Hule had one hand up to shade his squinted eyes against the glare of the reddening sun riding on their shoulders. The other hand gripped a Colt Paterson.

"Bowen! Who the…? Well I'll be double-damned."

He let loose with two short, shrill whistles. A dozen more Rangers blossomed in the brush on all sides. No doubt about it, mused True, they were as good at using sparse cover as wild Spanish cattle.

Steelman clambered up the sandy cutbank and came to stand beside Hule, brushing off his trail-grimed preacher's coat. He took one look at True and shook his head.

"Should have killed you the last time. I don't make the same mistake twice." He turned his flinty, killer-gray gaze on Chance. "What happened to Lon?"

"Dead. They put about a pound of lead into him and left his carcass for the buzzards."

"Take any of the heathens with him?"

"Yes, sir. Two. Would've done for more, had he been carrying a Colt."

"The new gun would have drawn too much attention to you. At least he sent two of them to Hell. Why are you still alive?"

Chance nodded at True.

"So you have influence with the Comancheros," said Steelman flatly, peering at True. "I guess that's all the proof we need of whose side you're on."

"Think what you like. I didn't come here to chew the breeze."

"Why did you?"

"A trade. My brother, in return for Golden."

"Why don't I just take Private Bowen away from you?"

True took a long look at the dirty, haggard, grim-faced men surrounding him.

"Reckon you could. But then that would prove there's not two bits worth of difference between you and the Comancheros."

"Aw, hell," said Hule impatiently. "Let's just ventilate the little sonuvabitch and quit this jawin'."

He lifted the Colt.

Chance gadded his horse. As spur-iron bit deep, the animal lunged forward. True managed to hold onto the reins, which pulled the horse's head around. With his mount turned broadside to Hule and Steelman, Chance slipped boot from stirrup and kicked at Hule, hitting the burly Ranger slap in the chest. Hule lurched backward, but did not fall. Familiar with Hule's temper, Steelman spun about and barked, "Back off!"

"Whichever side he's on," said Chance, "he's still my brother."

Trembling with rage, Hule flicked burning eyes at Steelman, then lowered the pistol.

Steelman faced True again. "What are your friends doing on the other side of that rise?"

"Waiting."

"For what?"

"For you to make your play."

Steelman stared for a long minute—just about the longest minute in True's entire life. It could go either way, thought True. Everything depended on this man, and whether there was one small spark of integrity left in his body. A hard and bitter man, who perhaps still heard the screams of butchered loved ones in the pitch of the prairie wind. True braced for the worst.

Steelman's gun-metal gaze flicked to one of the Rangers.

"Jubal, go fetch the prisoner. And his horse."

"Cap'n, you can't…" began Hule.

Steelman's sharp gesture cut the other's protest off in midsentence.

The man named Jubal went down into the arroyo. As True took Sombra's knife from his belt and cut the rawhide thongs lashing his brother's wrists to the saddlehorn, Steelman stepped closer.

"Private Bowen, I'll thank you for your report."

That caught Chance off-guard. Collecting his thoughts, he slowly shook his head.

"Helltown is a tough nut to crack, Cap'n. Maybe a hundred and fifty Comancheros all told, counting women and children. No Comanches shown up, yet. The place is a damned fortress. I think we'd need an army to take it. Reminds me of the Alamo, sir. A hundred and eighty Texans held off five thousand of Santa Anna's soldiers for thirteen days."

"Thank you, Private, for the history lesson."

"I'm just sayin', Cap'n, that Helltown looks a lot like the Alamo to me, and just as hard to take."

Steelman grimly considered the bearded, sun-dark features of the men who had followed him fearlessly so many perilous miles. They had come far, and risked much, to fight and die for the Republic. Turning back now would go against their grain.

"You can destroy Helltown later, Captain," said True.

Steelman looked at him sharply.

"Later?"

"Sure. You know where to find it, now. Come back later. After I've got my sister back, I'll even help you."

"You?"

"That's right."

Hule barked a laugh.

"Turn around and head for home," suggested True.

"You forget. I have no home."

"All I need is time to get my sister back."

"Is your sister's life worth the life of Texas? The Comancheros must be stopped. And why would you want to help me anyway? You're one of them."

"I'm a Texan, by God!" said True fiercely. "And I'll fight the next man who says it ain't so!"

It may have been a smile tugging at the corner of Ben Steelman's mouth. No one knew for sure, as he killed it stillborn.

Jubal came up out of the wash, leading the shaggy zebra dun by its bit chain. Golden sat the saddle. His face lit up when he saw True.

"Well bless my soul. Sombra said you'd be comin' on."

"You all right, Golden?"

"Can't complain, as I'm still kickin'."

"You two are free to go," said Steelman.

"Come on, Golden." True turned the stallion, wishing to waste no time, lest Steelman have a change of heart.

"True." It was Chance.

True looked around, hopeful.

Chance opened his mouth to speak, then clamped it shut with a curt shake of his head.

"Never mind."

True tapped his heels and the white launched into his grand pace. Golden had to put the dun into a high canter to keep abreast.

"What's going on, True?" he asked as they rode out of the trees and up the long *loma* slope.

"Don't honestly know. But I don't think we're out of the ditch yet."

"Life is one tribulation after another."

Reaching under his shirt, True fetched out the Bible and gave it back to Golden.

"Obliged," said the ex-pirate. "I shore missed havin' the Scripture to comfort me while in the midst of that pack of heathens."

"Oh, they ain't so bad."

They were clear to the crest of the grassy rise before they saw the Comanchero watcher come up out of the tall graze, rifle in hand, so close and sudden that their horses snorted and acted up. He pointed silently in the direction of the arroyo, and True looked in time to see the Rangers riding out of the trees.

They were heading in the opposite direction.

"I'll be," murmured Golden, amazed. "I never would've thought."

True didn't have a good feeling about it. Texas Rangers didn't give up that easy.

The Comanchero turned and loped to his pony, ground-hitched and cropping grass a little ways off. Way out yonder, True could see the rest of the Helltown crew, riding toward him. Sombra was out in front of the others, quirting the blaze-faced sorrel into a belly-down gallop and waving wildly.

Golden waved back.

"See you got a new horse, True," he remarked, as they rode to meet her.

He said it real casual, as though the white stallion was just another *mesteño*, and the fact that True was riding him was no great shakes.

True broke out laughing.

They put some miles behind them before making camp. Rodrigo Shay did not permit a fire until his outriders came in, the ones he had sent to shadow the Rangers for a spell. These men reported that the Rangers had not doubled back. Satisfied that there was enough ground between them so that a night attack by the enemy was out of the question, Shay relaxed. Buffalo chip fires were built. The night turned cold, but True didn't mind. He had Sombra to hold, and she kept him plenty warm. They watched the stars. The night was so clear and the stars seemed so close that they could see the colors in them, red and yellow and frost-blue.

Midmorning the next day, as they drew near the Cap Rock, a dark line across the western horizon, a rider came out to meet them. His foam-flecked horse was nearly windbroke from the long run. Shay went ahead to meet him. They talked a spell. The messenger gestured vigorously. Something was definitely boiling in the kettle.

As Shay rode back to True and Sombra and Golden, True felt his heart racing. Shay gave him a good hard look before speaking.

"A band of Comanches has arrived in Helltown. Black Wolf is among them."

End of the road.

16

Shay went on ahead with the rider who had brought the news from Helltown. True wanted to go along, but Shay was adamantly opposed to the idea. Before leaving, he spoke earnestly to a couple of Comancheros, pointing at True, and Sombra said he was probably giving orders that True be stopped, by any means necessary, if he tried to follow.

That put True on the prod. "He can't tell me what to do. He doesn't own me. I'm free to do what I want."

"There are all kinds of freedom," remarked Golden. "For instance, those Comancheros are free to kill you if they want to."

Sombra touched True's arm. "I know you are eager to see your sister. But we must abide by the rules. If you go charging in there, making trouble, the Comanches will probably get angry and leave. Believe me, True, this is the only way."

True grimaced and watched Rodrigo Shay ride away.

They reached Helltown by midafternoon of the longest day in his life.

As they ascended the trail from the sweetwater springs to the rim of the arrowhead mesa, Sombra offered more advice.

"The Comanches will have raised their tepees along the road. We must pass through their camp. Even if you see your sister you must promise you will not stop and make trouble."

"Don't rightly know if I can do that."

"Do you love me?"

"You know I do. What does…?"

"Then trust me. If you do not do as I say, we may lose our only chance to get Sadie back."

True nodded bleakly.

"Promise me," she insisted.

"I promise."

"Good. I know you will not break your word. Not you."

There were about thirty tepees pitched on both sides of the road, about ten rods from the Helltown gate. Made from buffalo hides on a framework of sixteen long poles, they stood, on the average, twelve feet high. The hides were stained yellow from the smoke of countless willow-wood fires. All the doors, covered with deerskin or bearskin, faced east, away from the high plains wind.

Seeing Comanches again gave True a bad time.

There were men, women, and children in the camp, maybe four-score in all, and most came to line the road and watch the riders pass. Some of the Comancheros knew the lingo, and exchanged greetings with this or that warrior. True got the impression this was done out of courtesy; that the relationship between Indian and trader was mostly business, and that they tolerated each other only because it was in the best interests of both to do so.

Sombra and Golden rode on either side of True, and he noticed the brace of Comancheros directly behind were keeping an eagle eye on him, and had their hands on the butts of their pistols.

The Comanche warriors had their lances, bison-hide shields, and Osage-orange bows in hand. Some few carried rifles. But they weren't done up for the warpath, for their faces and the tails of their ponies—held in a cavvy west of camp—were not painted carmine red.

The women wore buckskin dresses. Most of the children were naked. The men, for the most part, wore only breechclouts, though True did see a couple wearing shirts, another a pigeon-tail coat, and one a dented stovepipe hat, set at a jaunty angle on his head. These articles of white men's clothing, True felt sure, had been taken from dead Texans in last summer's raid on the Republic.

A great deal of attention was paid to the white stallion. A ripple of excited comment stirred the crowd. They knew the legend. There was only one White Pacer.

True didn't recognize any of the warriors, until he passed Black Wolf.

He knew him right off. He still wore that wolf-jaw necklace. A single black feather dangled from his scalplock, and side braids of hair were tightly wrapped in fur.

And he remembered True. His dark broad face might have been carved from stone, but his black eyes, unblinking, latched on and followed True as he rode by. They glittered with hostility. True figured his survival had to be a mark against Black Wolf. The warrior looked like he wanted a shot at doing the job right.

True's heart sank as he neared the Helltown gate. He had not seen Sadie among the savages.

The gate was opened for them, and closed behind. As the gun crew dispersed into the crowd milling in the plaza, Rodrigo Shay descended a ladder from the pole platform high up on the west wall, from which he had watched their arrival.

As True slipped off the back of the white stallion, Shay came forward to lay a hand on his shoulder.

"You did well, True. I know how difficult it must have been."

"I didn't see her."

"All the white captives are being kept out of sight."

"Have you seen them?"

He shook his head. "To ask would have been improper."

"When does the trading start?"

"Tonight there will be a great feast. We will present our guests with gifts of whiskey and tobacco. Then tomorrow we get down to business."

"I've waited this long. Reckon I can wait one day more."

With that, he brushed past Shay and climbed the ladder to the platform.

As night fell a bonfire was built between Helltown's west wall and the Comanche encampment. Its flames leaped as high as the walls of the Comanchero stronghold. Other, smaller, cookfires were made around it. Several dogs were killed, gutted, and beheaded, the hair singed off, and what was left boiled in big kettles. A couple of colts were also butchered, and prime cuts were put on sticks and roasted.

Sombra stayed with True on the platform throughout the night. She didn't say much. She didn't have to; it meant a lot to him, her just being there.

The Comancheros brought out many jugs of whiskey to pass among their guests. They gave the busthead away by the *carreta*-load. True remarked to Sombra that this seemed to be all give and no take. She smiled and shook her head.

"Good business, True."

Quill Eason had joined them for a spell. Now he seconded Sombra's comment.

"That's what it is, all right. Indians drink that rotgut like it was water. May not hold their liquor very well, but they can sure put it down. A couple of jugs tonight, and they'll wake up in the morning ready to trade their grandmothers for more. Just pure panther juice, and cheap enough to make. A little alcohol cut with red peppers, gunpowder, molasses, and a pinch of strychnine."

"Sounds strong enough to kill."

"Sometimes does."

Before long the effects of the whiskey became evident. Some of the warriors commenced to yelling and jumping around the fires like men who had bedded down on an anthill. One buck toppled into the fire. He came out screaming, hair and breechclout on fire. A pair of Comancheros knocked him down, rolled him in the dust, and managed to put him out. Someone came and threw a blanket over him, and then everyone seemed to forget about him. He was left to lie there for hours before several squaws came to cart him off.

A number of warriors raced their ponies up and down the road, trying to perform horseback tricks at full gallop. They might have put on a splendid show, had they not been stinking drunk. As it was, they survived falls that would have killed or crippled sober men.

A few of the Comancheros mingled among the Indians, but True noticed they weren't drinking much at all. Just enough to be sociable. Their eyes were keen and clear as they watched the crazy-drunk Comanche make fools of themselves.

Quill asked about the run-in with the Rangers. When True told him they had headed east, away from Helltown, Eason shook his head and gazed way off beyond the firelight, like he was expecting something or someone to appear suddenly out of the darkness, coming hard.

True asked him if he regretted killing that Goliad banker man, and as a result having had to throw in his lot with the likes of these Comancheros.

"Well, if I could choose my partners, they wouldn't be first on the list, True. But we don't always get to choose, do we? And, hell, I ain't sorry about Rutherford. I'd have been sorrier had I *not* done him in. I reckon by killing him I did Texas a favor. He was a cheat and a scoundrel and, in my book, responsible for the murder of a good and decent man. But I guess we could never make Ranger Hule see it that way."

"I reckon not."

"An eye for an eye. A life for a life. Those are old rules, tried and true. Hule and I both live by them. We aren't so different. And we'll soon settle the matter once and for good."

"Right and wrong depends on what side of the fence you're standing on," reflected True.

Quill laughed that I-don't-give-a-damn laugh of his.

"Good luck tomorrow, True Bowen. I got a feelin' you'll make it through. Good night, ma'am."

A while after Quill left, Golden appeared. True was looking through the pirate eyeglass, as he had been almost constantly since climbing up onto the platform. He scanned the crowd gathered round the fires, and searched the night shadows among the tepees farther out. He hadn't yet caught a glimpse of Sadie, and had to keep telling himself, over and over again, that she *was* down there, somewhere. She just had to be.

"I'd be honored to speak for you tomorrow, True," said Golden.

"What do you mean?"

"I know enough Comanch' to get by. First light, if you'll allow me, I'll go to Black Wolf. Tell him someone wants to dicker. Then I'll set in at the haggle and translate."

"I'm obliged."

"My pleasure. You want to start with the *manada* we caught?"

"No. Offer the white stallion."

Golden looked down into the plaza. All night the stallion had stood beneath the platform.

"You sure?"

True nodded.

Looking at the stallion, Golden shook his head, and murmured, "Beats all I ever did see. You two stayin' up here till dawn?"

"Reckon so."

"God bless you, boy. Your sister's lucky to have a brother like you."

"I let her down once. I'll not again."

The day broke clear and warm.

True kept thinking about the homesteaders who had laid claim to their dreams in the fertile river valleys of the Republic of Texas; about how they were probably out this fine spring morning, tilling their fields and laying in this year's crop. And he could visualize them throwing anxious looks into the distance, with their rifles primed and ready on their backs, or lashed to their plows, wondering when dream-shattering death and destruction would come sweeping down off the high plains again. He thought about this, and the more he thought about it, the more he hated Helltown—and what it stood for.

Below, the gate opened, and Comanchero women emerged carrying four buffalo robes, which they laid out, side by side, in the middle of the road. Rodrigo Shay followed. He sat in one of those heavy velvet-upholstered chairs, near the robes. The brace of Comancheros who had carried the chair stood arrayed behind him, bristling with artillery. Shay stretched out his legs, crossed them at the ankles, folded his hands in his lap, and tilted his head to gaze into the blue dome of the sky.

"All trading will be conducted in the presence of my father," explained Sombra. "Should a dispute arise, he will settle it. His decision is final. There is no appeal. If his word is not obeyed, by either party, the two men behind him will kill the violator."

Golden walked out through the gate, and down the road into the Comanche camp. A warrior intercepted him. They spoke for a moment. The warrior led the way to one of the tepees. A moment later Black Wolf emerged from the tepee. Watching the conversation through the telescope, True had to remind himself to breathe.

Behind him, Helltown's plaza was coming to life. Cookfires were stoked in the *brasseros*. Dogs barked. An infant squalled. Dust rose in a choking roan-colored cloud from the mustang corral.

Warriors began to leave the Comanche camp, trailed by squaws carrying hide- or blanket-wrapped bundles on their backs. Some of the braves weren't able to walk straight, suffering the morning-after effects of the potent Indian whiskey. They sat cross-legged in the vicinity of Shay and the buffalo robes. The squaws spread the bundles out in front of the warriors, and traders emerged from Helltown to examine the plunder the Comanches had to offer.

What he saw then turned True's blood cold.

Few Texas pioneer families were well-to-do, by any means. But almost every wife had brought a couple of belongings in the move that were precious to her. In many cases these treasured items were family heirlooms, passed down from generation to generation. A set of silverware, a gold brooch or ring, a Sunday go-to-meeting dress or a wedding gown, a hand mirror, a book or two, lace curtains, quilts, a few select pieces of glass or china.

All these things True saw as the bundles were untied. All that, and more. Watches, boots, pipes, ropes, tools, family Bibles, gold coin and paper money in small quantities, a corset, a pair of spectacles, a fiddle, a French harp, even a sampler. God Bless This Home And All Who Enter Here.

The Comanches were proud of their bloody harvest. All True could think about were the good folk who had once called these things their own. Good people, tortured, scalped, murdered.

Also among the stolen goods were flat stones the size of a man's palm. A few of these were painted vermilion red. True asked Sombra what these stones signified.

"The painted stones represent white captives the Comanche are willing to trade away. The others indicate how many mules or horses they have for trade."

"They exchange horses for horses?"

"Sometimes. Most of the horses the Comanches steal are trained to the trace. They prefer mustangs. Look!" She pointed. "There's Golden."

He was coming out of the Comanche camp. Drawing near the wall, he motioned for them to join him.

Slipping the eyeglass under his belt, True took hold of Sombra by the shoulders.

"Whatever happens, are you with me?"

"*Para siempre.*"

Forever.

He climbed down off the platform and walked through the gate, Sombra beside him, the stallion right behind.

17

She was wearing a buckskin dress, ornamented with beads and the long fringe Comanches favor. Her mahogany brown hair, once so long and luxuriant, had been hacked short. Her face was painted like a Comanche woman's, with yellow lines on the eyelids, and small red circles on either cheek. But her eyes were as cornflower blue as True remembered them. Bold and bright and brave eyes.

Sadie.

She was walking down the road, several paces behind Black Wolf. True wanted to run to her. He took a step without realizing it. She shook her head sharply, looking right at him. Seeing her alive filled his heart with indescribable joy.

Black Wolf swaggered to the buffalo robes, and stopped across from True. As Sadie came along behind, he turned on her, pointed to the rutted red dirt of the road and barked a harsh command. She started to sit down. He yelled at her, and cuffed her viciously with the back of his hand. She took this abuse with stoic silence, and sat with eyes cast down. Some of the other warriors laughed and spoke to Black Wolf, who looked at True with an arrogant smile.

True drew a long breath and stayed put.

Golden stood at his shoulder. "He claimed she was moving too slow to suit him, so he hit her. The other braves were complimenting him."

"A real lady's man," remarked Quill Eason.

Looking over-shoulder, True saw him standing among the Comancheros gathered at the Helltown side of the buffalo robes.

Black Wolf sat cross-legged. Golden did likewise so True followed suit, Sombra sitting close beside him.

"Let's get started," said True.

Golden said something to Black Wolf in Comanche, which sounded to True like the noise a person made choking on a chicken bone.

Black Wolf reached out and grabbed a handful of Sadie's hair, wrenching her head back. Her lips parted to show clenched teeth, and the muscles in her neck stood out as she strained against the painful hold. Black Wolf rattled on for a full minute. All the while, Sadie's eyes were fastened on True.

"He says he ain't sure he wants to trade her away," translated Golden. "Says she hasn't got enough meat on her bones to suit him, but she does manage to keep his blankets warm. Says several braves have tried to buy her from him. He has turned down the offer of many horses to keep her. It amuses him to have a wife different in so many ways from his other wives."

"Get on with it, Golden. Offer the white stallion."

As Golden spoke, Black Wolf let go of Sadie. His gaze lifted to the stallion standing behind True. He tried not to give his feelings away, but True could see the desire on his face.

When Golden was done, Black Wolf said his piece.

"He insists this cannot be the White Pacer," interpreted Golden. "No *taibo*—no white man—could catch the great white stallion."

True leaned forward. "Remind him that this *taibo* was the one he run a lance through last year, and I'm still alive. I took his best shot, and it just wasn't good enough."

Golden hesitated. "True, I don't..."

"Tell him. And tell him he knows full well this is the White Pacer. This is business, and no time for playing games."

Golden spoke. Black Wolf showed no anger. He was gazing at True in a speculative way as he answered.

"He says that he is, in fact, growing bored with her. She is too skinny and stubborn for his taste. He has tired of her disrespect. He can't beat it out of her. She is good for nothing. He might as well be rid of her.

"He also says he remembers you. Says you must have the spirit of the coyote in you. That's the only explanation for your survival. He admits it is possible that a parson possessed by the coyote spirit could have tricked the white stallion. The stallion is big medicine. It is fitting that a great warrior like Black Wolf possess this horse."

"You'd think the sun comes up just to hear him crow," muttered True.

Golden was grinning. "You done it, True. Now you get that stallion over here onto these buffalo robes, and the deal is done."

You done it, True.

Yes, by God. He had done it. He had Sadie back.

He was leading the stallion forward when Gancho appeared out of nowhere to block his path.

He hadn't changed a bit since their border town standoff. A tall, lean loafer wolf, blood red shirt tucked into pants that in turn were tucked into jackboots. He was grinning—the way an alligator grins.

Lifting his left arm, he put the iron hook right in True's face, and looked over at Rodrigo Shay.

"This gringo is a thief, *jefe*. He stole the white stallion from me. It is I who should be trading with Black Wolf for the woman."

"That's a dirty lie!" protested True.

"I have witnesses who will vouch for me. The white stallion is rightfully mine. Is that not so, Guerrero?"

"*Sí. Es verdad.*"

True looked around at Guerrero, the mustanger he had kicked through the cantina door that day. With him were the other *mesteñeros* who rode with Gancho.

"These are his men," True told Shay. "What do you expect them to say? You know he's lying. Ask Golden. Ask your own daughter. He's getting even with me because Sombra left him to help me."

Shay was inscrutable. His eyes were green ice.

"Gancho," he said, "you have made a mistake."

Gancho spun away from True. Three long, angry strides, and he was confronting Shay. The Comancheros behind Shay laid hold of their pistols.

"I tell you the stallion belongs to me!" roared Gancho. "The gringo stole it!"

Shay stood up slowly.

"Father, he is lying," said Sombra. "True *did* catch the stallion."

"How does she know this?" argued Gancho. "Was she with him? No! She was leading the Rangers to Helltown."

"Be careful with your words," warned Shay.

Gancho made an insolent gesture, and addressed the crowd of Comancheros standing in the blue morning shade of Helltown's west wall.

"It is my word against the Tejano's. Let the dispute between us be decided according to the law we live by here at Helltown. The law you made, Rodrigo Shay."

Someone shouted, "*La Cinta!*" Others took up the cry. True searched the crowd for Quill. Eason rode with Gancho. He could testify on True's behalf.

But Quill Eason had vanished.

Shay silenced the clamor with an upraised hand.

"True," he said, "you must decide. Either you give up the stallion to Gancho, or the two of you will fight. La Cinta is the way we settle disputes of ownership such as this, where one man's word stands against another's. It is a duel to the death."

"I'll fight," said True.

La Cinta. The Sash.

A fight to the death with knives.

The rules were simple. Gancho and True took *the* ends of Rodrigo Shay's scarlet sash in their teeth. If one of them let go of the sash for any reason, the two Comancheros flanking Shay would kill him.

The word spread like wildfire. Seemed to True as though every living soul in Helltown and the Comanche camp congregated to watch the duel. There was a great deal of wagering on the outcome. Gancho was the odds-on favorite.

Reacting to the tension in the air, the noise and excitement of the crowd, the white stallion went to fussing. At Shay's command, several mustangers unlimbered their reatas. Two put loops around the stallion's neck, and the third threw the forefoot *mangana*. This really boiled the stallion's water; he shrieked, lunged, twisted, and kicked. He dragged the mustangers into the press of onlookers, scattering the crowd like rousted quail. When he fell, they stretched him out and kept him down.

"Gancho's got you at a disadvantage, True," said Golden. "With that hook, he has two weapons to your one. Watch his knife, not his eyes. That was the lesson I learned when I got this." He traced the scar quartering across his face with a thumb.

The crowd formed a tightly packed circle. The Comanches were stirred up by the prospect of entertainment just to their liking. Gancho, confident of victory, wore a wolfish grin.

Stepping into the circle, True shucked the blanket-serape and wrapped it around his left arm, leaving some to dangle. Then he accepted the end of the scarlet sash Shay offered, stuck it in his teeth, and drew Sombra's knife from his belt.

Shay stepped back to the rim of the circle.

"Begin."

Gancho hooked the sash and pulled downward, slashing at True with his knife at the same time. Yanked forward, off-balance, True almost fell into the arc of the blade. Sweeping his own knife in a desperate, backhand motion, he caught Gancho's knife against his own and fended it away.

They circled, crouching. Gancho feinted with the knife, struck with the hook. True ducked under. The iron grazed his scalp. Again Gancho slashed with the knife. This time True spoiled the thrust with the blanket-serape. Gancho's entangled blade rent the fabric and came free. He swung the knife at True's face. True caught the blade with his own, as before. Steel clashed against steel. True deflected another jab and stepped in, throwing a punch that struck

Gancho in the neck. Gancho answered by lashing out with the hook. True cast up an arm to block the blow. The hook bit deeply, tearing flesh and muscle below the shoulder. Falling, True clutched the sash with his left hand. Gancho had to bend forward or lose his grip on the sash. He locked his legs to keep from pitching forward. True scissor-kicked one leg out from under his opponent. Toppling sideways, Gancho ate dirt.

As he tried to rise, True pulled back, still grasping the sash, and Gancho sprawled. True kicked him in the face. Growling, Gancho lunged. They grappled, rolling this way and then that in the dust. Gancho got him pinned down and tried to crack his skull with the hook. True twisted his head out of the way and threw a leg up into Gancho's back, shoving Gancho forward into another brutal punch. Blood sprayed from Gancho's nose. The blow rocked him sideways, and True pitched out from under.

Dazed and bleeding, they both got up and began circling again. Gancho had lost his confident grin. They slashed and feinted and parried, blades ringing together, casting sparks, steel flashing in the sun, red dust swirling around them. True found he could still use his injured arm; he could feel the blood streaming, but no pain. Yet. His sleeve was soaked. His jaw ached like the dickens from clenching the sash so tightly in his teeth. He kept jerking his head back, trying to catch Gancho off-guard and pull the sash from his adversary's teeth. Gancho did likewise. They acted like two dogs contesting a bone.

True didn't care for his prospects, figuring that Gancho knew more about knife-fighting than he ever would. So far he'd been lucky. He couldn't rely on luck to get him through, though. He had to outsmart Gancho. But it was difficult to think calmly and clearly. The crowd was howling for blood. True watched Gancho's knife, waiting for the next thrust, hoping he could avoid it, wondering what would become of Sadie if he failed.

Gancho charged forward, swinging the knife low and the iron hook high. True jumped back, and Gancho kept coming, plowed right over him. Falling, True wedged his knees up into Gancho's belly and catapulted the mustanger over his head. Both men rolled to hands and knees, got up, and slammed into one another like a pair of rutting bulls. The crowd gasped, thinking this was surely the end. True felt cold steel slice his left side, just below the ribs. His own blade gashed Gancho's hip, grating off bone.

Gancho reeled away. They stood, half-crouched, three feet apart, the sash taut between them, heaving in air and bleeding all over the place. The crowd cheered. What fine sports, hacking each other to pieces!

But the crowd fell abruptly silent when True cut the sash in half with one quick slash of the knife.

He backed away, to the edge of the crowd. Rough hands pushed at his back.

Gancho was stunned by this unexpected development. He spat the end of the sash out of his mouth.

"Coward!" he railed. "Stinking gringo coward!"

True glanced at Rodrigo Shay.

He still had his end of the sash between clenched teeth.

Shay's shamrock-green eyes glittered with comprehension.

"You have lost, Gancho," he declared

"What? Are you loco? What do you mean? He cut the sash!"

"Yes. But you *let go* of it."

Gancho stared at Shay, at True, and finally at the length of scarlet cloth curled like a snake at his feet.

"There is nothing in the rules of La Cinta which prohibits the cutting of the sash," said Shay. "Perhaps there should be. It has never happened before. Maybe I will amend the rules. Tomorrow. But, for now, you have lost, Gancho."

"Bastard!" cried Gancho, his face an ugly, congested mask of hate.

He flipped the knife to catch it by the blade, and reared back to hurl it at Rodrigo Shay.

The two Comanchero bodyguards fired their pistols as one.

The bullets struck Gancho squarely in the chest, throwing him backward. His heels drummed against the red hardpack, his body twitched, and then his head lolled sideways, dead eyes staring.

Sombra shoved through the press of spectators and threw her arms around True's neck.

"You'll get blood all over you," warned True.

"I don't care!" she cried, ecstatic.

Shay approached them, a hand extended.

"My congratulations, True. Let us be partners. Join me. You are entirely too clever to have for an enemy."

True looked him square in the eye.

"We *are* enemies, Shay."

A crash of gunfire came from the direction of the Comanche camp. Shouts of alarm filled the air. The crowd scattered. True saw riders galloping hell-for-leather through a drift of dust and gunsmoke.

Texas Rangers!

18

Comanchero women and children fled through the gate into Helltown. Some of the men did, too. Others stood their ground to return fire. The air was filled with the whine of hot lead. A bullet came close enough that True could hear it shimmy, and he promptly threw Sombra to the hardpack, shielding her with his body.

Shay stood nearby, peering quizzically over the west wall at the belfry of the chapel. True knew what he was wondering, and wondered the same. Why hadn't the lookout raised the alarm?

"Get down!" True yelled at him.

He looked at True, scowling, then spun on his heel and walked toward the gate. He didn't hurry one bit; acting for all the world like a man out for a stroll. One of his bodyguards went down. A heartbeat later Shay was hit.

True saw the bullet strike, the puff of dust off his buckskin jacket, high up in the back near the shoulder. The impact turned him around. He faced the gate again, took two steps, and dropped to one knee, head bowed, as though he were praying.

"Father!"

Sombra knocked True over in her scramble to reach Shay. At the same time, True heard Sadie call out to him.

He whirled. A few of the Comanches were firing back at the Rangers. Others—including the women and children—were running for the cavvy of ponies, some distance away. More shooting came from that direction; the Rangers had hit the herd, too.

Black Wolf was dragging Sadie by the arm, and she wasn't going peaceably.

True took off running. Black Wolf, seeing him, yelled to another warrior, who turned, notching an arrow to his bowstring. True didn't break stride. Pulled the knife from his belt and hurled it. No hand at knife-throwing, he got the Comanche high in the arm. The warrior reeled, shooting the arrow into the ground. True hit him full out. Both men went sprawling. Both men bounced to their feet. The Comanche, having dropped his bow in the collision, pulled the Spanish knife out of his arm and advanced on True, who was now unarmed. He walked right into a bullet that put him down for good.

True retrieved the knife. Black Wolf was still struggling with Sadie. She was on the ground, kicking and clawing. With a disdainful gesture he gave up on taking her, screamed a taunt at True, who was coming on at a sprint. Then he turned and ran.

Falling to his knees beside Sadie, True took his sister in his arms.

"True," she breathed. "I knew you'd come for me someday. I never gave up hope."

He couldn't say anything. Just knelt there, holding her tight.

The thunder of hooves brought his head up. A Ranger checked his lathered mount in a spray of dirt. He was bringing his Colt to bear on Sadie.

"No!" yelled True hoarsely. "She's not Comanche!"

The Ranger wasn't listening. Blood-crazy eyes burned in a face flushed with the fever of battle. True didn't have time to do anything except push Sadie to the ground and fall on top of her.

Chance came riding out of the dust, gut-hooking his horse straight into the mount of the Ranger. The Ranger went down with his horse. He got up, stumbling like a drunkard, and went down a final time with an arrow jutting from his chest. Chance fired one shot, killing the Comanche twenty yards away who had fired the arrow.

As the Ranger's horse got up, True lifted Sadie off the ground and into the saddle. Gathered the reins and put them in her hands. The horse pivoted, and True backed away. Sadie reached for him.

"Come on, True!"

"I can't. Chance, take her out of here."

Chance looked at Sadie, his face a blank, powder-blackened mask.

"Dammit, Chauncey!" yelled True. "Don't you go lookin' at her like that! She's our sister."

The mask fell away, and True saw the Chance Bowen he had known long ago.

"Don't call me that," said Chance—and smiled.

Putting his horse broadside to Sadie's, he reached out to grab hold of the bit chain.

"I'm not letting you out of my sight this time, Sis. True, pick up that Colt and climb on behind Sadie, so's we can get the hell out of here." He threw an anxious look around, and shook his head. "'Fore it's too late."

True picked up the fallen Ranger's repeating pistol.

"I'm not leaving without Sombra."

"Can't you talk sense to him?" Chance begged Sadie. "You were the only one who could before."

Searching True's face, Sadie smiled faintly. "He knows what he's doing."

"I'll catch up," said True. "Now git!"

Sadie threw one last look over her shoulder as they rode away into the swirling haze.

The Comanche tepees were burning now, and a dense wave of smoke, carried on the high plains wind, broke against the west wall of Helltown. The Comancheros were withdrawing through the gate, firing steadily at a dozen Rangers charging headlong across the hardpack now littered with dead and dying men and horses. More Comancheros appeared on the platform where, the night before, True had kept his vigil. Crashing gunfire was an unrelenting thunderclap. True started for the gate. A swarm of bullets seared the air around him. He dropped behind the body of a dead Comanchero.

Half of the Rangers were shot out of their saddles almost immediately. Theirs was a gallant, hopeless charge. Horses went down shrieking. The gate closed on a pile of dead Comancheros. The rest of the Rangers came on, yelling and shooting. The riflemen on the platform fired another devastating volley. Only one Ranger reached the wall alive, shooting at the men above him. A Comanchero came cartwheeling down. The Ranger fired point-blank at the body as it fell past, and then he too was hit. Another bullet creased his horse, which took off at the gallop, dragging the Ranger, whose boot was caught in the stirrup.

The shooting became sporadic. In the lull, True heard Comanche warcries off in the distance. They were busy, for the moment, trying to get their women and children to safety, and fighting Rangers for possession of their horse herd.

True got to his feet, turned toward the sound of hooves striking the hardpack. Out of the fog of gunsmoke and dust and smoke from the burning Comanche camp came the white stallion.

The horse had worked free of the forefoot loop, and was trailing the other two ropes from his neck. True figured when the shooting started the *mesteñeros* who had been keeping him stretched out must have dropped their reatas and hauled freight for cover.

The stallion didn't care for the ropes on his neck, so True stuck the Colt in his belt and used Sombra's knife to cut them off. The stallion whickered and nudged True with his muzzle.

"Yeah," said True, grinning. "I'm glad to see you, too."

Big iron hinges creaked as Helltown's main gate opened. Three riders emerged, holding their horses to a walk.

Sombra and Golden, with Quill Eason.

True swung aboard the stallion and went to meet them.

"Your father?" asked True, pulling alongside Sombra.

"Alive."

"The war ain't over yet," said Quill. "The Comanch' will be back, with a hankering to spill Texican blood."

"That includes you," Golden told True.

"So you must go," added Sombra. "And I'm going with you."

"I'm going with her," said Golden, pointing his thumb at Sombra.

"I'm just going," grinned Quill.

❧   ❧   ❧

Pausing at the sweetwater springs, near the bottom of the trail descending from the arrowhead mesa, they washed the smokeburn out of their eyes and soothed parched throats. As they anticipated a hard run ahead, they let the horses drink only sparingly. Quill hunkered down at the rim of the pool to fill his canteen, and True joined him.

"You're taking a big chance," said True.

"Well, it's not like I'm going to chaperone you folks all the way back. Soon as we get shut of this canyon I'll make my own tracks."

"Why'd you do it, Quill?"

"Do what?"

"Somebody took care of the lookout."

"Think you're pretty smart, don't you?" He laughed. "You can see why I couldn't stay in Helltown. When the dust settled someone was bound to remember seeing me head into the chapel right before the shivaree started."

"You're not telling me why."

"Decided maybe I *did* have a choice, after all. Maybe I'm no better than a Comanchero. Maybe I *am* a murderer, but I'm still a Texican. Your people are my people. So I got rid of the lookout. Everybody else was busy watching you and Gancho cut each other to ribbons. Speaking of which, you'd better have that pretty woman of yours tend to you, hoss, before you bleed plumb to death."

"No time for that now," said Golden, coming over. "We gots bad company."

He pointed to the plume of dust rising from the mesa rimrock high above them.

Capping the canteen, Quill rose.

"You'd think there had been enough killin' for one day, now wouldn't you?"

19

Unfortunately for Quill, they ran into the Rangers—or what was left of the Rangers—before they got out of the canyon.

Steelman and five of his men were holed up in a gully that cut across the gorge. Their bottomed-out horses stood with heads lowered and sides billowing. Most of the men were wounded, one mortally. The front of his chest was a bloody frothing mess, and his ragged breathing was frequently interrupted by a wracking cough as he hacked up pieces of torn lung. Another man held his hat over the dying man's face, providing a small circle of shade. The sun blazed directly overhead, and it was quite warm and still in the canyon, where the prairie winds did not reach.

Here, the gorge narrowed, and there was no way to get around the Rangers unseen.

True angled the white stallion to ride in beside Quill.

"Maybe they won't know you by sight," he said.

"Sure they will, True. I'm a papered man. Hule will, for sure."

"Maybe Hule's dead."

"Maybe it's Christmas." Quill flashed his ne'er-do-well grin. "Don't fret too much on my account. Hule and I may as well settle our differences. This is as good a place as any to die."

Sadie came running out of the gully. True jumped off the stallion and caught her in his arms, swinging her around. Then he spotted Steelman and Hule approaching, and let go of her, stepped in front of her, his hand resting on the butt of the Colt Paterson in his belt.

"Howdy, boys," called Quill. "I hear tell you been lookin' high and low for me. Well, here I am."

"Heel yourself, you bastard," growled Hule, reaching for his gun.

True had his pistol drawn, aimed, and cocked before Hule could clear his own Colt.

"Don't."

"This man is a criminal," declared Steelman, referring to Quill. "Your helping him makes you one, Bowen."

Chance came out of the gully. He strode past Steelman and Hule, and walked right up to Eason, who was still mounted.

"You're under arrest, Quill Eason. Handover your iron."

"Not just yet."

"Stand away, Private Bowen," warned Hule.

"This man is my prisoner," snapped Chance. "I'm taking him in, alive."

"Now that sounds like a real honest-to-God Ranger talking," said True.

"We've got a passel of irate Comanches and their Comanchero friends on our backsides, gentlemen," said Golden. "Mebbe we should save our ca'tridges for them. If, an hour from now, any of us are left alive, then you boys can get to killing each other off."

"Fair enough," said Steelman. He looked with mild scorn at Hule. "At ease, Sergeant. By thunder, I'm sick to death of having to keep you on a short rope."

He wheeled and stiff-legged it back down into the gully; he had taken a bullet in his left thigh. A bandanna bound the wound. Every other step he took, True could hear blood squishing in his boot.

"When this is over," Chance told Quill, "I'll expect your gun."

With a lazy smile, Quill touched the brim of his hat.

When they were all down in the gully, True begged Golden to take Sombra and Sadie and skedaddle.

"Are you stayin' put?" asked Golden.

True nodded. "If we can keep them bottled up in this canyon for a spell, you three might get away clean."

"I'm not leaving my brothers," declared Sadie, having overheard.

"And I'm not going anywhere without you," Sombra told True.

"Look, maybe we can slow them down here, but we can't stop them. There are just too many. Sooner or later they'll ride right over us."

"Perhaps there won't be as many as you think," said Sombra.

"What does that mean?"

"Perhaps it will only be Comanches."

"Your father's got to help Black Wolf. If he doesn't, Helltown is finished."

"Well, I sure ain't ridin' out all by my lonesome," shrugged Golden. "So I reckon we'll all be staying put."

True didn't argue. He could see it would be a waste of breath. In a poor frame of mind, as he did not feature any of them surviving, he sought out Ben Steelman. The Ranger captain was sitting with his back to the gully's bank, loading up his Colt.

"Hope you're satisfied," barked True, mad enough to spit smoke. "A lot of men have died, and a lot more are fixing to."

"We've killed many Comanche. And a lot of Comancheros. The more we kill, the better off Texas will be. That's our job. If you don't like the odds, you're free to move on."

"You owe Quill Eason thanks, by the way. He took care of the Helltown lookout this morning. Otherwise, you wouldn't have gotten as close as you did before being discovered. He knew, somehow, that you were going to circle back around and attack. When I told him the Rangers had headed home, he didn't buy it."

"We didn't come all this way to turn around and go back. We'll make our stand here. Our horses have given out. Better to fight here than to be caught out in the open. Leastways, here they can't outflank us. They must charge straight down the barrels of our guns."

"There were white captives in that Comanche camp, Captain. One of your men almost killed my sister, taking her for an Indian. Makes you wonder what happened to the other prisoners, don't it?"

"If they were killed, then they are better off."

True shook his head. "You're a hard man, Captain Steelman. Do you still hear them scream?"

He jumped. "What?"

"Never mind."

"*Here they come!*" someone yelled.

"If you prefer a long gun," said Steelman, "your Hawken is tied to my saddle. Powderhorn and bullet pouch, as well."

True fetched the rifle. Back at the gully bank, he looked up-canyon and saw them, five hundred yards off. He couldn't make out much except a lot of dust boiling up.

"You men spread out," yelled Steelman.

"Carney's dead," said the Ranger who had been shading the face of the lung-shot man. He clamped his hat back on his head.

"He missed a good fight. Nobody fires until I give the order."

"How many you reckon?" asked Hule, on the other side of Steelman from True. He wasn't worried, just curious.

"Enough so's every man can strike a blow for Texas," replied Steelman.

At four hundred yards the Comanche spotted their prey and started yapping like a bunch of moonstruck coyotes. True loaded the Hawken.

Golden came up. "I ain't got a gun, True."

He held the Bible in one hand, and took the Colt that True offered with the other.

Steelman held out a handful of cartridges. "Better make sure it's fully loaded. Might not get a chance to reload."

As Golden loaded the Colt, True said, "I'd be obliged were you to stay close to the womenfolk, Golden."

Golden nodded. Watching him move away, True realized that the white stallion was standing right behind him.

"You're gonna get your fool head blowed off."

The stallion whickered.

On True's left, Chance said, "You always wanted to fight Injuns, brother."

The Comanches were two hundred yards away.

True remembered the lance going clean through his mother. And little Meg's screams as the Comanch' tossed her around like a jug of corn liquor. And Ernest, impaled on another war lance, held high in the air. He remembered it all, clear as yesterday. Just as clear, he could hear Sadie's cries as Black Wolf ran him through with a lance.

Hard to forgive and forget.

He could see Black Wolf now, riding a spotted pony, out in front of the pack of screaming hostiles.

Thumbing dust off the front sight, True lifted the Hawken, nestled the inscribed butt-plate into his shoulder.

Drew a bead on Black Wolf.

"This is for the Bowens," he muttered, and squeezed the trigger.

He was blinded briefly by white powdersmoke. When next he looked, he saw the spotted pony... but no Black Wolf.

"I said wait for my command to fire," snapped Steelman.

"Got a long gun here, Captain," replied True, reloading, having now to raise his voice over Comanche noise. "Mind if I put it to good use?"

Steelman either grimaced or smiled. True wasn't certain which. Then, lifting his Colt, he yelled, "Fire!"

The crash of gunfire was deafening. It kept on and on, as the repeating pistols talked death. Firing the Hawken again, True scarcely heard the boom of the .53-caliber long gun. The gully was quickly filled with powdersmoke, burning the eyes and smelling like rotten eggs. True lost sight of the Comanches altogether for a moment. Reloading as quickly as he could, he did not see the mounted warrior until the latter reached the rim of the bank directly above. True was still tamping down the charge, and fired without removing the ramrod. The ramrod pierced the Comanche's neck, flying straight out the back in a spray of blood. The pony was rearing, and the warrior somersaulted off its rump.

Another Comanche launched himself off the bank and took Chance to the ground. The warrior was lifting his knife for a killing blow when True shattered the stock of the Hawken against the back of his skull. Chance hurled the dead redskin away, lifted his Colt and fired. Another warrior rolled down the embankment, shot through the heart.

Two arrows struck Ben Steelman in the chest. He staggered, the hammer of his Colt falling on an empty chamber. A Comanche hurtled off the bank and drove his lance through the Ranger captain. Yelling like a madman, Chance charged past True, emptying his pistol into the warrior. He ran right into the path of a war pony diving off the bank. The collision knocked him twenty feet. The horse went down, throwing its rider. The Comanche rolled to his feet and made for Chance, who lay face-down and unmoving in the sand. True tackled him, and drove Sombra's Spanish knife into his back.

The shooting suddenly slacked off.

True reached Chance just as Quill did. Together, they rolled him over. True was relieved to see Chance move a little, and groan. His arm was broken. A fragment of bone jutted out of his torn, blood-soaked sleeve.

"He'll live," said Quill, and smiled.

"*Eason!*"

Quill was only just starting to turn when the shot rang out. The bullet threw him across Chance's body and into True, knocking True backward.

Ranger Hule stumbled out of the swirling smoke and dust. The Colt slipped from his fingers. When he fell forward on his face, True saw the arrow driven deeply between his shoulder blades.

He had saved his last bullet for Quill Eason.

Quill's eyes were half-closed. His face was ash-gray. He was still smiling.

"Never thought he'd shoot me in the back."

"I ain't surprised," said True.

"Don't hear the guns. Did we win?"

"Reckon so."

"Good for Texas," were Quill Eason's last words.

❧ ❧ ❧

Except for Chance, all the Rangers were killed. They took twenty-six Yamparika Comanche with them. True figured that suited them just fine.

Only a handful of warriors lived to run away from the canyon fight. As the smoke thinned, True spotted a passel of Comancheros, fifty or more, sitting their horses way up the gorge. The Comanches passed by them, and the Comancheros just sat there. All but one rider. As this one neared, True recognized Rodrigo Shay.

He sat a tall horse at the top of the gully's bank, his shoulders bunched. Still carrying Ranger lead, he looked bad. But when he saw Sombra, standing beside True, he took a turn for the better. He surveyed the carnage briefly and then, with a curt nod, wheeled his horse around and returned to his men.

"Well," said True, amazed by the turn of events, "that's the end of Helltown, ain't it? When word gets out your father left Black Wolf to fend for himself, the Comanch' won't have anything more to do with him, will they?"

"He'll survive," said Sombra, not without pride. "He always has."

Watching the Comancheros disappear around a bend in the canyon, True figured they would all be dead for sure, had Rodrigo Shay not loved his daughter as much as he did.

Using pieces of a Comanche war lance for splints, True set his brother's arm. Golden, having accounted for three Comanches on his own, had taken an arrow through the calf of his leg. Snapping off the feathered end, he had pulled the rest of the shaft out and used the hot barrel of his empty Colt to cauterize the wound.

True could not abide leaving brave men to the buzzards, so Golden helped him dig shallow graves in the sandy bank. They used lances and their bare hands. Here they laid Steelman and his Rangers to rest, sitting up and facing east, toward the Republic they had given their lives for. Quill Eason, too. They covered the bodies with rocks. Afterward, Golden sang ' "Rock of Ages." Sadie chimed in, and True gave it a game try as well, though he could not carry a tune in a bucket.

Chance was conscious, but rattled. When they'd mounted up, True rode beside him, ready to catch him if he blacked out.

True left the Staked Plains on a Ranger horse, for the white stallion was gone. Vanished. He had seen him last right before the Comanche had swarmed into the gully. Golden said that the stallion, being a sight smarter than most people, had lit out once the shooting started. True spoke up in defense of the white, arguing that there wasn't a yellow bone in the stallion's body.

"I ain't talkin' about cowardice," answered Golden. "I'm talkin' about good ole horse sense."

True nodded sadly.

As that long and bloody day drew to a close, they rode out of the canyon, the dying sun at their backs.

Look for these reissued ebook titles by Jason Manning:

HIGH COUNTRY SERIES
- High Country
- Green River Rendezvous
- Battle of the Teton Basin

FLINTLOCK SERIES
- Flintlock
- The Border Captains
- Gone To Texas

TEXAS SERIES
- The Black Jacks
- Texas Bound
- The Marauders

MOUNTAIN MAN SERIES
- Mountain Passage
- Mountain Massacre
- Mountain Courage
- Mountain Vengeance
- Mountain Honor
- Mountain Renegade

FALCONER SERIES
- Falconer's Law
- Promised Land
- American Blood

ETHAN PAYNE SERIES
- Frontier Road
- Trail Town
- Last Chance

THE WESTERNERS
- Gun Justice
- Gunmaster
- The Outlaw Trail

TIMOTHY BARLOW SERIES
- The Long Hunters
- The Fire-Eaters
- War Lovers

APACHE SERIES
- Apache Storm
- Apache Shadow
- Apache Strike

OTHER TITLES
- Showdown at Seven Springs
- Texas Helltown
- Texas Gundown
- Gunsmoke on the Sierra Line
- Revenge in Little Texas
- Robbers of the Redlands (originally titled Texas Blood Kill)